CULTURES OF THE WORLD

IRAQ

Susan M. Hassig

MARSHALL CAVENDISH
New York • London • Sydney

Reference edition published 1993 by
Marshall Cavendish Corporation
2415 Jerusalem Avenue
P.O. Box 587, North Bellmore
New York 11710

Editorial Director	Shirley Hew
Managing Editor	Shova Loh
Editors	Tan Kok Eng
	Leonard Lau
	Siow Peng Han
	MaryLee Knowlton
Picture Editor	Yee May Kaung
Production	Edmund Lam
Art Manager	Tuck Loong
Design	Ang Siew Lian
	Ong Su Ping
Illustrators	Lo Chuan Ming
	Kelvin Sim
Cover Picture	Gerard Champlong (The Image Bank)

Printed in Singapore

Originated and designed by
Times Books International
an imprint of Times Editions Pte Ltd
Times Center, 1 New Industrial Road
Singapore 1953
Telex: 37908 EDTIME Fax: 2854871

Library of Congress Cataloging-in-Publication Data
Hassig, Susan M., 1969–
    Iraq / Susan M. Hassig.
        p. cm.—(Cultures of the world)
    Includes bibliographical references and index.
    Summary: Discusses the geography, history, government,
economy, and culture of the country where the world's first
civilization was born.
    ISBN 1-85435-533-3 (vol.) :   —ISBN 1-85435-529-5 (set)
    1. Iraq—Juvenile literature.   [1.Iraq.]   I. Title.
II. Series.
DS70.6.H35 1992
956.7—dc20
                                            92–12178
                                               CIP
                                               AC

INTRODUCTION

IRAQ IS A POLITICALLY VOLATILE COUNTRY that has dominated the world's headlines for the past few years. It is a republic headed by President Saddam Hussein, a man who is hated and feared by people of all nations. Unfortunately, the negative image of the country's leader has affected the public's opinion of the Iraqi people. Unlike their president, the people of Iraq are good-natured, loyal and trustworthy people.

The world's first civilization was born in ancient Iraq, or Mesopotamia. Humankind's first cities and government institutions originated in Mesopotamia, or the "land between two rivers." The topography of the country varies from vast deserts in the south, to marshy regions surrounding the rivers, to rugged mountains in the northern region of Iraq.

As part of the series *Cultures of the World*, this book about Iraq will teach you about the Iraqis, their customs, religious beliefs, artistic interests, language and lifestyle. It will enable you, the reader, to disregard the media images displaying an evil nation and learn about the truly remarkable citizens of this country.

Iraq

Mesopotamia

Euphrates

Tigris

● Baghdad

CONTENTS

Along the Shatt al-Arab, where the Tigris and Euphrates meet, fan-shaped date palms stretch as far as the eye can see.

CONTENTS

Baghdad is the city of legends. It is home to Sindbad, Aladdin, Ali Baba and the magic carpet.

GEOGRAPHY

ONCE KNOWN as the historic country of Mesopotamia, the Republic of Iraq is located in southwestern Asia. Iraq's neighbors are Turkey to the north, Syria and Jordan to the west, Iran to the east, and Kuwait and Saudi Arabia to the south.

Iraq is completely surrounded by land except for a 25-mile wide outlet at the southeastern tip of the country where it meets the Persian Gulf. The total land area of Iraq is approximately 173,588 square miles in addition to one-half of the 1,408-square mile neutral zone shared with Saudi Arabia.

Ancient Iraq was called Mesopotamia, meaning "land between the rivers." This name was chosen to describe the twin-river system and river valleys of the Tigris and Euphrates. The two rivers originate in the mountains of eastern Turkey and flow past northern Syria before coming down to the lower valleys of Iraq.

The Tigris and Euphrates rivers provide life-sustaining water for irrigation, yet threaten the country during spring when floods frequently occur. The land around the river is fertile and produces abundant wheat and other crops.

Beyond this fertile area, the topography and vegetation of Iraq drastically change. The country becomes a vast, dry desert in the southern region and a cold, mountainous landscape in the north.

Opposite: **On the road to Basra, an important oil refining center and Iraq's only port city. Basra lies beside the Shatt al-Arab river which drains into the Persian Gulf.**

Above: **Iraq lies in the heart of the Middle East.**

7

A Kurdish settlement in northeastern Iraq. This mountainous region is a favorite summer holiday destination because of its cool weather and scenic beauty.

FOUR GEOGRAPHICAL REGIONS

The geographical history of Iraq is over 5,000 years old. In ancient times, Iraq was the site of the world's first-known civilization which thrived on the rich plains between the Tigris and Euphrates. The fertile soil must have encouraged wandering nomads to settle down and create organized communities. But if the rivers did not have systems to control the flow of water the land could be destroyed by massive floods. The dual nature of the rivers has caused many civilizations, such as Sumer, Assyria, Babylonia and Akkad, to thrive or not according to the floods.

The different topography, climate and vegetation allow geographers to separate Iraq into four distinct regions: the Delta Region, the Steppe-Desert Plains, the Northern Foothills and the Kurdish Country.

THE DELTA REGION The Delta Region is the southeastern portion of Iraq between the capital city, Baghdad, and the Persian Gulf. Most of the land in the Delta Region is a broad alluvial plain. In the south near Basra, where the Euphrates forms a marshy lake called the Hawr al-Hammar, is an area of many channels, canals and lakes. A visitor to the Delta Region is usually mystified by the never-ending lakes, dense foliage and seemingly prehistoric "marsh-dwellers."

The Tigris and Euphrates meet in the Delta Region and form the Shatt al-Arab. Along its banks lies Iraq's only port, the city of Basra. Most Iraqis reside in this region and their lifestyle varies from the simple "marsh-dwellers" to the sophisticated residents of the larger cities.

THE STEPPE-DESERT PLAINS The area west of the Delta Region is the Steppe-Desert Plains. Most of the area is part of the arid Syrian Desert. Vast reaches of the plains are devoid of people. A person could stand here and look in all directions without seeing any life or vegetation. The topography of the Steppe-Desert Plains is a combination of sand and stony plains. A few channels of the Euphrates run through this region. However, they are dry for most of the year.

THE NORTHERN FOOTHILLS The region located north of the city of Samarra and between the Tigris and Euphrates is the Northern Foothills. This region of grassy plains and rolling hills receives generous rainfall. Although few trees are found here, the foothills produce an abundance of grain and, unlike the Delta Region, the area experiences cooler summers and colder winters. The Northern Foothills are the site of many archeological remains, including the ancient city of Assyria.

THE KURDISH COUNTRY Northeastern Iraq is a mountainous region inhabited mainly by the Kurds, a non-Arab people. The Kurdish Country is a beautiful and popular summer vacation spot, but is bitter cold in winter. The terrain consists primarily of mountains, valleys, terraced gardens and hill-pastures. The Kurds reside in the valleys and foothills where they cultivate the soil. The mountains serve as a haven for rebels and criminals. This region differs from the other geographical areas not only in topography, but also in culture, language and tradition.

The marsh region by the banks of the Euphrates. Known as marsh dwellers, the Iraqis who live here build reed houses on little islands dotting the Hawr al-Hammar.

9

Floods still occur when there is heavy rainfall. Cities by the Tigris and Euphrates often experience flooding when the rivers overflow and break through the walls holding back the rivers' rushing waters.

CLIMATE

The climate of Iraq differs dramatically among the four regions. Northern Iraq is temperate in the summer and freezing cold in winter. The eastern and southeastern areas experience tropical climate with high humidity, while the western area has a dry, desert-like climate. Nationwide, temperatures in the summer average from 72 F to 110 F, while in winter temperatures dip to near freezing in the north and to 60 F in the south.

During the summer months between June and September, Iraq is visited by a northwesterly wind, the *shamal*. The *shamal* is a dry and dusty wind that lasts for as long as several days and is often accompanied by duststorms. Few clouds are formed and the burning sun produces high temperatures. In winter, the south and southeast are visited by the *sharqi,* a cool and moist wind blowing from the sea.

Iraq is a very dry country with relatively little rainfall. Much of the rain falls in the winter months while summers are very hot and dry. The annual rainfall in Iraq is approximately 16 inches in the Delta Region and between

15 to 25 inches in the Northern Foothills and Kurdish Country. The rain evaporates quickly in all regions of Iraq. Thus Iraqis must depend upon irrigation to cultivate the soil. On the rare occasions when the rainfall is heavy, destructive floods occur.

FLORA

More than 30 million date palms, each producing about 1,000 dates during its fertile years, grow in Iraq. Dates are a sweet and popular fruit; 50% of their weight is attributed to their sugar content. Dates are Iraq's largest agricultural export. Over 80% of the world's supply comes from Iraq. In

Harvesting dates, a dark and extremely sweet fruit which is exported all over the world. Dates are especially popular in Middle Eastern countries where they are used in a variety of food and desserts.

addition to the fruit, other parts of the palm tree can be used. The palm fronds are used for weaving and the fruit pits are ground into a beverage. Due to the many uses of the date palm, Iraqis refer to it as "the eternal plant" or "the tree of life."

In the higher elevations of Iraq, such as the Kurdish Country, alpine plants grow naturally. These plants are able to withstand the freezing winters. Oak, maple, juniper and hawthorn trees also thrive in the mountains of Iraq.

A large portion of Iraq is desert. The flora of this area is able to survive the dry summer months and then bloom profusely in the spring to provide food for the animals and to propagate. The desert vegetation of Iraq is similar to the vegetation in the states of Arizona and New Mexico.

Along the Tigris and Euphrates, reedy marshes exist. The reeds of these plants are used commercially by the cosmetic, drug and food industries.

FAUNA

For its size, Iraq has relatively little wildlife. One of the most common mammals in Iraq is the camel. The camel is a strong desert animal that can exist on very little water while traveling over great distances. Camels are domesticated and trained to carry heavy loads across the desert.

Although the vast deserts of Iraq appear to be void of life, they are actually inhabited by a variety of wildlife which normally appear at night. Two of the most common creatures of the Iraqi desert are lizards and snakes. Other wild desert animals include the hyenas, jackals and gazelles.

The mountainous regions of northern Iraq are the residence of several types of predatory animals such as wild bears, leopards and wolves.

The Tigris and Euphrates contain a variety of freshwater fish that are caught for food. Birds, such as ducks and geese, reside near the rivers or swampy marshes. A very common bird in Iraq is the stork which often nests on the roof of private houses. The owners of the house believe that they will be blessed with good luck if a stork chooses to nest on their home.

THE WORLD'S OLDEST CIVILIZATION

According to the Moslem, Christian and Jewish faiths, God created the world in six days and rested on the seventh. The first man and woman were Adam and Eve and they lived in the Garden of Eden. The site of the Garden of Eden, humankind's first habitat, is believed to be in southern Iraq.

In addition to being the reputed site of the birth of humankind, Iraq is the home of the first known civilization. In the middle 19th century, archeologists uncovered the ancient cities of Mesopotamia and discovered ruined buildings, clay tablets and pottery. By studying these ancient artifacts, archeologists are able to understand how people lived and organized their society.

RURAL IRAQ

Although 70% of Iraqis now live in the larger cities or their surrounding suburbs, many people still reside in rural areas where life is guided by local tribal customs. The villages, or tribes, are usually run by a sheikh ("SHAY-k") who lives in the largest villa in the area. Because of his age and wealth, the sheikh often has up to four wives and many children.

The other villagers live in small houses made of mud bricks. The roofs are thatched from twigs or reeds and the dirt floors are covered with woven rugs. In most households, elderly parents live with their eldest son and his wife and family. Other family members live in nearby houses.

The villages' economic base is agriculture. Therefore, most villages are built on the fertile land along the Tigris or Euphrates. The people depend on the water for irrigation and cannot survive without it.

To a city-dweller, rural people may appear to be backward. Many have not adopted Western-style clothing and still wear traditional Iraqi costume. Women are isolated from the men, and sometimes polygamy is still practiced.

METROPOLITAN IRAQ

BAGHDAD Between the banks of the Tigris and Euphrates lies Iraq's capital city of Baghdad. Baghdad is located in the Delta Region and has a population of approximately 3,600,000 people.

The city is a beautiful mix of the old world and the modern world. Karkh district, located on the west bank of the Tigris, is the modern section and is filled with ultra-modern high rise buildings and elegant avenues. Rusefeh district, on the other hand, is the ancient part of the city complete with narrow, dusty streets and outdoor bazaars.

Baghdad was a small village until A.D. 762 when it was chosen by an Islamic leader as his headquarters. By A.D. 800, Baghdad had become a

A view of Baghdad by the banks of the Tigris. In addition to housing a large majority of the population, Baghdad is the center of economic and political authority.

populated city of culture and education. Baghdad continued to prosper until it was almost totally destroyed by invaders in 1258. In 1932, Baghdad was chosen as capital when Iraq gained its independence from the British.

Today, Baghdad is the home of the government, Iraq's chief industries, an airport and several universities.

BASRA Iraq's chief port in the Persian Gulf is the city of Basra. Basra is Iraq's second largest city and is located approximately 75 miles from the Persian Gulf. During the war with Iran from 1980 to 1988, Basra's many oil fields were a prime target. As a result, much of Basra was destroyed and a large majority of the population fled for safety. However, in the past few years Basra has regained its control of Iraq's oil exports and its inhabitants have returned.

MOSUL Mosul is Iraq's third largest city and serves as the center of northern Iraq. It is located on the west bank of the Tigris in Kurdish Country. The majority of Mosul's residents are Arab or Kurdish Moslems, though the largest Christian community also resides here. Mosul depends on oil, cotton, grain, fruit and sheep for commercial prosperity. Because of the abundance of cotton, weaving is a popular craft in Mosul.

KIRKUK Iraq's fourth largest city, located in the northeastern region, is the city of Kirkuk. Kirkuk serves as a major hub for the oil industry. The countries of Syria, Lebanon and Turkey have oil pipelines that begin here and run to the Mediterranean Sea. The population of Kirkuk has increased rapidly as more Iraqis have moved from the countryside to the cities in the past few decades.

15

HISTORY

THE WORLD'S FIRST KNOWN CIVILIZATION began in Iraq in approximately 4000 B.C. Mesopotamia, the ancient name of Iraq, witnessed the rise of Sumer, a group of 13 city-states in the area between modern-day Baghdad and the Persian Gulf. Sumer thrived as a cultural region that gave birth to writing, mathematics and science.

The Akkadians, led by King Sargon I, conquered Sumer in approximately 2334 B.C. After 200 years, the Sumerians once again rose under the king who ruled Ur, a city in the east. The new empire was short-lived as new conquerors moved into Mesopotamia.

The Babylonians conquered Mesopotamia in 1900 B.C. and ruled until approximately 1600 B.C. The sixth ruler of Babylon, King Hammurabi ("ham-moor-A-bee"), developed an extensive legal code that was the most comprehensive collection of laws at that time. Known as the Code of Hammurabi, it covered issues of family laws, criminal laws and civil laws.

The last of the great civilizations to develop in Mesopotamia was that of the Assyrians. The Assyrians were led by a firm and ruthless monarchy that controlled Mesopotamia and the neighboring country of Syria. Besides being known for their fighting prowess, the Assyrians were also monumental builders as the excavations at Nineveh, Ashur, Khorsabad and other sites have shown. By the early 7th centurry B.C., revolts by the Chaldeans of southern Sumer put an end to the Assyrian regime. Perhaps the most famous Chaldean king was Nebuchadnezzar II ("NEH-buhk-ad-nehz-zahr") who reigned from 605 to 562 B.C. He was known for his military might and the magnificence of his capital, Babylon.

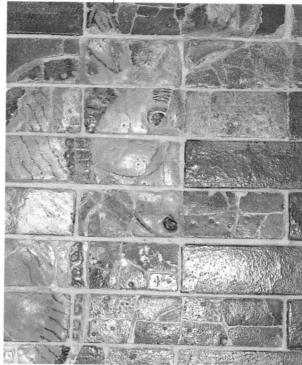

Opposite: **Enclosed in the courtyard of possibly the largest mosque in the world, this spiral minaret was built during the Abbasid caliphate.**

Above: **These blue-glazed tiles, with a relief of a bull, once belonged to the Ishtar Gates that protected Babylon from all invaders.**

FOREIGN CONQUESTS AND INFLUENCE

After the Chaldeans, a new history in Mesopotamia began as foreign civilizations invaded and conquered the country.

The first were the Persians who conquered the region and added it to their empire in 550 B.C. The area remained under Persian rule until Alexander the Great conquered the region in 331 B.C. The Greeks introduced metropolitan cities, scientific rationalism, improved irrigation systems, trade and commerce. Alexander had wonderful plans to restore the old temples of Babylon, but died of malaria at the young age of 32 before his plans were completed. His successors were weak and the Greeks soon lost Mesopotamia to the Persian Parthians in 126 B.C.

For about 300 years, Mesopotamia was controlled by the Parthians, migrants from Turkestan and northern Iraq. The invaders were true fighters who overthrew Greek rule, but retained the cities and the culture of their Western predecessors. For a brief period, from A.D. 98 to 117 and again from A.D. 193 to 211, the Romans occupied Mesopotamia. The Parthians managed to regain control until A.D. 227, when the Iranian Sasanids swept in from the east.

One of the most important conquests of modern-day Iraq occurred when followers of the Islamic Prophet Mohammed, in A.D. 636, led troops into Mesopotamia and began converting the Christians to Moslems. By A.D. 650, the Iranian Sasanids had been thoroughly defeated and Mesopotamia became the Islamic state it is today.

THE GOLDEN AGE OF IRAQ

One of the greatest periods in Iraqi and Islamic history occurred during the Abbasid caliphate from A.D. 750 to 1258. The Abbasid caliphate was led by a descendant of Mohammed named Abd al-Abbas. The followers considered themselves to be blessed by Allah to rule the country.

The rulers of the Abbasid caliphate were called caliphs. Under the reign of the caliphs, Iraq experienced a Golden Age. The city of Baghdad was built as a round city of three sections. The people resided in the outer ring, the army in the second ring and the rulers in the center. Baghdad became the capital of Iraq and was the center of political power and culture in the Middle East. Iraq developed as an important trade center between Asia and the Mediterranean Sea because Baghdad was an open market for all countries.

The Golden Age was slowly replaced by an economic decline. The Abbasid caliphs spent too much money on the rapidly growing cities and not enough on the rural areas. Eventually, the profits of the cities diminished and prosperity ended.

Iraq was overrun by Mongol hoards that came streaming down the plains of Central Asia and sacked Baghdad in 1258. The Turks seized Mesopotamia in the 16th century and the region became part of the Ottoman empire.

Baghdad reached its peak of glory under the rule of Caliph Harun al-Rashid. Great monuments, such as this Askari Shrine in Samarra, were built. It was during Harun al-Rashid's reign that *The Thousand and One Nights,* a collection of Arab folktales, was supposedly put together.

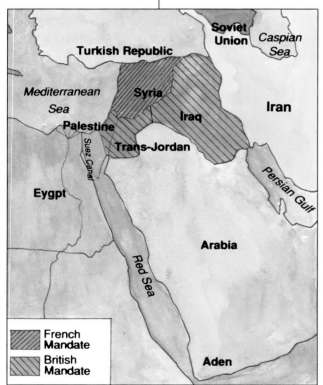

French Mandate

British Mandate

After World War I parts of the Ottoman empire were assigned to the victors by the international League of Nations. Iraq and Palestine came under British Mandate while Syria and Lebanon were administered by France.

THE BRITISH MANDATE

In 1917, during World War I, the British invaded and captured the city of Baghdad. By 1918, they invaded Mosul and claimed all of Iraq save the Kurdish region in the north. The British conquest of Iraq was to balance the German presence in Turkey. The British feared that their enemies, the Germans, would possibly harm and even control communication and oil lines between Britain, the Middle East and India. In 1920, a mandate was formed that created an Iraqi Arab State. The British Mandate was unsatisfactory to the citizens of Iraq and they planned several unsuccessful revolts.

INDEPENDENCE

In October 1932, Iraq was admitted to the League of Nations as an independent monarchy. With its independence, Iraq experienced many problems from both neighboring countries and internal confrontations. King Faisal ("FY-suhl") ruled the tumultuous country of Iraq until his death in 1933.

The throne was turned over to his son, Ghazi, who was unable to pull the divided country together. Ghazi's rule was interrupted by a military coup, yet he remained in control until his early death in an automobile accident in 1939. His infant son, Faisal II, became the new sovereign ruler of Iraq. Until Faisal II was old enough to rule, Ghazi's cousin Amir Abd al-Ilah ("ahbd al-ILAH") assumed the throne.

KING FAISAL II

Between 1948 and 1958, Faisal II was officially the King of Iraq. During his reign, the country was badly affected by World War II and his own political mistakes. In the late 1940s, the economy plummeted due to worldwide shortages and a mass exodus of 120,000 affluent Jews from Iraq to Israel.

On July 14, 1958, an uproar began in the streets of Baghdad as the people of Iraq revolted against the monarchy. The revolutionists, led by Abdul Karim Kassem, publicly executed King Faisal II, Amir Abd al-Ilah and other members of the royal family. This revolution was one in a series of military coups that plagued Iraq until the successful retention of power by the Baath ("ba-ARTH") Party in 1968.

The Martyrs' monument, dedicated to all who died fighting for their country.

Monument to the Baath Party who took control of Iraq in a bloodless coup in 1968.

MILITARY COUPS

In 1963, the Kassem regime was replaced by the Baath Party which orchestrated a military coup that lasted for less than a year. The party's lack of definitive programs and leaders permitted the Nasserites, a group led by Abd as-Salaam Arif, who had played a leading role in the 1958 revolution, to overthrow them. In 1966 Arif was killed in a helicopter crash and his militarily-weak brother, Abd ar-Rahman Arif, became president. In 1968, a highly organized and militarily strong Baath Party dominated by Saddam Hussein and Ahmad Hassan al-Bakr overthrew the president and established control of Iraq. Ahmad Hassan al-Bakr became the next president of Iraq and his nephew, Saddam Hussein, was named vice-president of the country and deputy secretary-general of the Baath. In 1979, Saddam Hussein became the president of the Iraqi Republic, a position he retains today.

HISTORY OF THE BAATH PARTY

Two Syrian students named Salah ad-Din al-Bitar and Michel Aflaq founded the Baath Party in the early 1940s. The students developed a political party based on the ideals of freedom, socialism, unity and a secularized government. The ideals of the Baath Party became ingrained in the minds of a few Iraqis during a wave of communism in the 1950s.

By 1955, the Baath Party had grown to approximately 300 members. The membership of the party grew in 1958 as many Iraqis became disgusted with the communist policies of the Iraqi leader, Kassem. The Baath Party continued to increase its strength and membership and today it is still the dominant party in Iraq.

THE IRAN-IRAQ WAR

In February 1979, Ayatollah Sayyid Ruhollah Musavi Khomeini ("ho-MAY-nee") overthrew the Shah of Iran. The new Islamic state threatened the power of the secular Iraqi government. After assassination attempts on top Baath officials and uprisings in religious groups, Saddam Hussein sent his troops into Iran for a full-scale war that lasted eight years.

The Iran-Iraq War commenced August 2, 1980, and finally ended in August 1988. Due to the political changes then, Iraq had invaded a disorganized Iran. Saddam hoped to quickly overrun Iran and replace it as the leader of the Persian Gulf. For the first few months of the bitter war, Iraqi forces laid siege to several Iranian towns and killed hundreds of troops.

The Iranians gathered strength and retaliated in the spring of 1982 forcing the Iraqis to retreat. Underestimating the new strength of the Iranian troops, Saddam attempted to settle the war. The bitter Iranians refused his peace offering and stormed Iraq's city of Basra, killing many Iraqis in the process.

The war continued and the death toll exceeded 18,000 by 1983. During a 24-hour period in 1984, over 25,000 soldiers were killed in a battle near Basra. Neither side would withdraw although death tolls continued to rise on both sides.

In 1986, the Iraqis used chemical weapons against Iran and killed over 10,000 Iranians. In retaliation the Iranians scored a near victory in a fierce attack on Basra. After hundreds of thousands of casualties, Khomeini and Hussein agreed to a cease-fire in August 1988 with neither country emerging as the victor.

THE GULF WAR

On August 2, 1990, Saddam Hussein sent Iraqi troops into Kuwait to seize the country and overthrow the monarchy. Executions, hangings and rapes became an everyday occurrence as the Iraqi armed forces ravaged Kuwait. Although hostility had been mounting between the two countries for some time, the world was shocked by the invasion.

In the months between August and January 1990, the United States, the Soviet Union, Japan, European nations and several Middle Eastern countries formed an alliance against Iraq. The United Nations authorized the use of force against Iraq unless its troops withdrew from Kuwait by January 15, 1991.

The deadline passed and on January 17, 1991, the Allies began an air attack on Iraq. The armed forces consisted of troops from the United States, Saudi Arabia, Britain, Egypt, France, Pakistan and Syria. The Allies staged a strategically planned air war against Iraq and Saddam Hussein, who claimed his country was "invincible."

On February 24, the 100-hour ground war began as Allied troops moved into Kuwait. Iraq withdrew, but it has been estimated that over 100,000 Iraqis lost their lives in a war that their leader still claims as a victory.

Opposite: **Two Iraqi soldiers lie dead in front of a scarred T-72 Soviet-made tank after combat with the U.S. infantry and armored divisions.**

Above: **Against a smoke-darkened sky, a U.S. marine waves the Kuwaiti flag as his battalion prepares to leave for home.**

GOVERNMENT

THE REVOLUTIONARY COMMAND COUNCIL (RCC) is the executive government of the Iraqi republic. The chairman of the RCC, Saddam Hussein, is also the president of the country. The RCC is a branch of the Baath Party (Arab Socialist Resurrection Party). All members of the RCC are also members of the Baath Party.

The Baath Party seized control of Iraq in a military coup in 1968. Since then, the RCC and the Baath Party have tried to build a single Arab nation under a socialist regime. At the present time, the strongest political leader in Iraq is Saddam Hussein. Saddam serves as president of Iraq, chairman of the RCC, commander of the armed forces, prime minister and secretary-general of the Baath's Regional Command.

In 1980, the RCC created the 250-member National Assembly to serve as the legislative branch of the government. The National Assembly is responsible for approving or rejecting laws proposed by the RCC. Its members are elected by a secret ballot every four years. To be approved for membership, a candidate must have Iraqi parents, an Iraqi spouse, proof of birth in Iraq and the ability to demonstrate the RCC ideals. The qualifications create a National Assembly that is essentially loyal to the RCC.

The judiciary of the Iraqi Republic is also controlled by the RCC. The judges of the appellate courts in Baghdad, Basra, Mosul, Kirkuk and Babylon are appointed by the president of Iraq. The courts rule over criminal, civil and religious matters.

Opposite: **After the Gulf War, Saddam Hussein turned his attention to the Kurds who were fighting for an independent Kurdish nation. These Kurdish refugees in Turkey were forced to flee from their homes to escape persecution.**

Above: **A loyal Iraqi citizen beside a portrait of Saddam Hussein.**

THE PROVISIONAL CONSTITUTION

In 1970, the Baath Party created the Provisional Constitution as the official governing law for Iraq. The constitution has two specific goals: a socialist system and Arab economic unity.

The constitution provides the right to personal property if the ownership is within the confines of economic prosperity for society as a whole. Personal property may be seized by the government if it is in the best interests of society and the owner is compensated in some way. Under the constitution, every citizen has the right to a free education up to university level, equal employment opportunities and access to free medical care.

The constitution allows the right to a fair trial, freedom of speech and freedom of worship. Citizens are also allowed the freedom to form parties based on political ideals. However, many of these safeguards have been flouted in persecuting Iraqis who oppose the regime.

28

THE LIFE OF SADDAM HUSSEIN

Saddam Hussein was born in a small, impoverished village on April 28, 1937. Saddam was raised by his mother and a cruel stepfather. The defiant Saddam faced his stepfather's frequent beatings like a man until he left home to attend secondary school in Baghdad. After living in a small village without electricity or water, Saddam embraced the big city of Baghdad and the political ideas of his uncle, Khairallah Talfah, with whom he lived for several years.

In 1957, the young Saddam joined the little-known yet politically active Baath Party. His loyalty was tested when other members of the Baath Party instructed him to murder Kassem, the leader of Iraq. Saddam and four others shot Kassem, but did not kill him. The rebels were forced into exile for several years until Kassem lost his power.

When he returned to Iraq, Saddam was thrown into prison for attempting to overthrow the government. While in prison, he studied the memoirs and works of Adolf Hitler and Joseph Stalin. Upon earning his freedom, Saddam quickly rose to his current status of president by ensuring that any other contenders for the position were either killed or frightened away.

LOCAL GOVERNMENT

Iraq is divided into 18 regions, each ruled by an appointed governor. The regions are comparable to the individual states of the United States, except the governors in Iraq are elected by the president instead of by popular vote. Within each region, there are several districts that are administered by appointed district officers. Each district is further divided into a subdistrict that is governed by a subdistrict officer. Finally, the individual cities and towns are governed by an appointed mayor. Saddam Hussein appoints the mayors of the important cities such as Baghdad, Basra and Mosul.

The different administrative districts of Iraq.

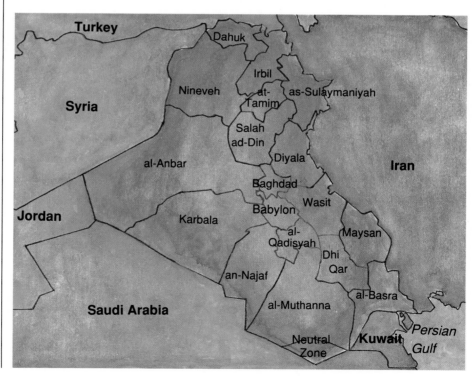

THE IRAQI ARMY'S REPUBLICAN GUARD

At the heart of the Iraqi armed forces lies the Republican Guard. This formidable group is the strength behind Iraq and was the main target of Allied forces during the Gulf War. It began as a small group of bodyguards for Saddam Hussein. While most special divisions are formed within the armed forces, the National Guard was born out of a group of men fiercely loyal to Saddam Hussein and the Baath Party. They became the country's top fighters.

Members of the Republican Guard led the destructive invasion of the neighboring country of Kuwait on August 2, 1990. The soldiers are educated men from middle- to upper-class families. Many members of the Republican Guard attended university, live in houses funded by the government, enjoy the luxuries of fine food and drink, and receive scholarships from the Baath Party to send their children to the university. Its soldiers receive so many benefits from the Baath Party and Saddam Hussein that they remain loyal fighters until death.

The Republican Guard is made up of eight armored infantry divisions of approximately 150,000 men. Trained by the former Soviet Union during the Iran-Iraq War, its soldiers are brilliant artillery, armor and air defenders. After the eight-year war with Iran, the Republican Guard became Iraq's elite army.

During the Gulf War, members of the Republican Guard were able to withstand incessant bombing by the Allied air forces as they were protected by massive fortifications. They also survived the Allied invasion of Kuwait air forces as Saddam ordered their withdrawal back to Iraq to protect the country's borders against a possible invasion.

The Iraqi army turns out in full regalia during a state celebration.

Only old men, women and children remain behind in many Kurdish towns. Many Kurds have either fled to neighboring countries or have been killed by Iraqi forces.

KURDISH AUTONOMY

The Kurds in the northern region of Iraq have demanded autonomy, or self-rule, since Iraqi independence in 1932. In 1970, the Kurds and the Iraqi government agreed on Kurdish autonomy for the three Kurdish regions and the surrounding Kurdish-inhabited areas. Although the initial agreement was made, the Kurds were unhappy with their limited power and war with the Iraqi armed forces followed.

During a military offensive in 1988, over 5,000 Kurds were killed with poisonous gas. The Kurds were forced to agree to the 1970 Autonomy Agreement. The region now has an Executive Council and a Legislative Assembly. The Executive Council is chaired by an appointee of Saddam Hussein. The remaining 11 members of the Executive Council are chosen by the chairman from the Legislative Assembly.

The Legislative Assembly consists of 50 members that are popularly elected by the Kurds. Prior to election, however, the candidates must be approved by the government. This allows Iraq to indirectly control Kurdish autonomy by approving only satisfactory candidates. The Legislative Assembly advises the Executive Council, ratifies laws and enacts legislation.

Kurdish autonomy does not exist in the minds of the Kurds. All of the important judicial, security, administrative and police decisions are still made by the Iraqi government. The Executive Council and Legislative Assembly are permitted to decide only insignificant matters. The lack of true autonomy may encourage the Kurds to break away and form an independent nation.

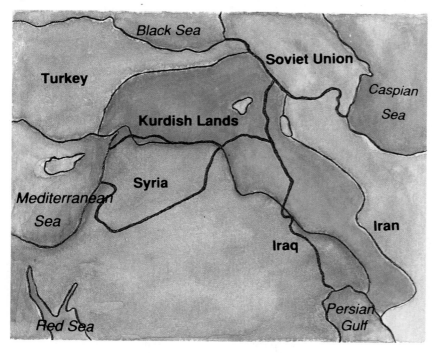

The Kurds inhabit an area spread over several countries including Iran, Iraq and Turkey.

ECONOMY

WHEN OIL BECAME THE PRINCIPAL INDUSTRY of Iraq in the 20th century, its economy surged. Iraq earned international status as one of the world's leading producers of oil and profited from sales to powerful nations such as the United States and the former Soviet Union.

The war with Iran interrupted Iraq's economic development. Many oil wells were destroyed in battle and profits dwindled. The government was forced to spend national funds on the purchase of military equipment. At the end of the war in 1988, Iraq's economy had hit rock bottom. Fortunately, after the cease-fire, the oil industry recovered and Iraq's economy picked up.

Two years later, after Iraq invaded Kuwait a trade embargo was imposed on Iraq. This means that other countries would not sell anything to or buy anything from Iraq. Today, the country is still recovering from this devastating blow to its national economy.

Opposite: **Oil rig workers drill for oil beneath the seabed.**

Below: **Flares of fire in the Persian Gulf caused by the release of natural gas. A valuable asset, gas reserves in Iraq account for nearly 20% of the world's total reserves.**

Transporting oil. During the war with Iran, two of Iraq's main export depots were destroyed. This severely curtailed Iraq's ability to export oil to the outside world. The Iraqis were forced to transport their oil via trucks across the bordering countries of Turkey and Jordan. Pipelines were subsequently laid between Iraq and Turkey to speed up oil exports.

THE PRINCIPAL INDUSTRY: OIL

In 1908, the British discovered oil in Iran. This profitable discovery spurred similar explorations in the neighboring country of Iraq.

In 1927, the Turkish Petroleum Company (TPC), controlled by Britain and the United States, discovered a rich oil well near the northern city of Kirkuk. The TPC was renamed the Iraq Petroleum Company (IPC) and was granted a 70-year exploration contract by the Iraqi government. By 1938, oil had become a major export commodity of Iraq.

After World War II, Basra and Mosul became popular oil drilling sites. By 1951, Basra, Mosul and Kirkuk were exporting almost 20 million tons of oil annually. Upset by the revenue earned by foreign companies, the Iraqi government demanded 50% of all oil profits. IPC continued to operate in Iraq until 1973 when the government nationalized the oil companies, paying $300 million for IPC's shares.

The Iraqi government then set up a Ministry of Oil and formed the Iraq National Oil Company (INOC) which is responsible for the overall management of oil production in the country.

THE POWER OF OIL

Iraq soon became one of the world's leading producers of oil. It is a member of the Organization of Petroleum Exporting Countries (OPEC), an organization formed in 1960 to control petroleum prices worldwide. OPEC has 13 members: Iraq, Iran, Kuwait, Algeria, Libya, Qatar, Venezuela, Ecuador, Indonesia, Gabon, Saudi Arabia, Nigeria and the United Arab Emirates.

During the 1970s, OPEC raised the price of oil, which caused severe oil shortages in the United States and other countries dependent on oil imports. However, it lost some of its power in the 1980s when efforts to control production failed and other countries began exporting or conserving oil.

Oil has become such a major part of the economy of Middle Eastern nations that countries are willing to fight each other for it. On August 2, 1990, Iraq invaded Kuwait over an oil dispute and over border disagreements with the latter.

This chart shows the oil and natural gas production of Iraq as compared with other Middle East countries in 1984. By 1987, Iraq was producing 2.8 million barrels of oil per day and exporting 1.8 million barrels.

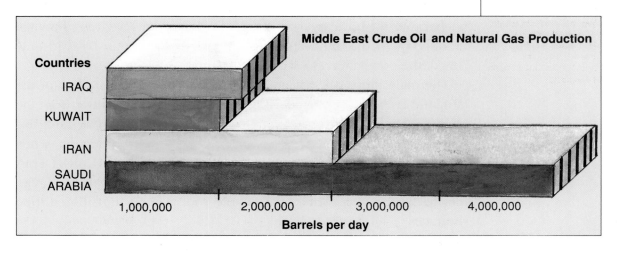

Middle East Crude Oil and Natural Gas Production

Countries

IRAQ

KUWAIT

IRAN

SAUDI ARABIA

1,000,000   2,000,000   3,000,000   4,000,000

Barrels per day

A small contributor to agriculture is the livestock industry. Animals raised in Iraq include sheep, goats, camels, horses and water buffaloes. The livestock is sold for the production of meat, fur and leather.

AGRICULTURE

Throughout its history, Iraq has been an agricultural nation. During the 1970s, almost half of the Iraqi labor force was involved in agriculture. As oil became the primary contributor to the country's Gross National Product (GNP), the emphasis on agriculture began to wane. By 1986, only 30% of the population still worked the land.

The main crops are wheat, barley, tobacco and dates. Most of the farmland is located near the Tigris and Euphrates. The water from the rivers enriches the soil for cultivation and provides irrigation for the crops.

The agricultural sector was forced to increase production when economic sanctions were placed on Iraq after the invasion of Kuwait. Prior to August 1990, Iraq imported almost 70% of its food. During the Gulf War, Iraq had to provide for its own people and, as a result, suffered food shortages.

WATER RESOURCES

For thousands of years, the Tigris and Euphrates have brought both joy and suffering to the citizens of the Delta. A plentiful supply of water has enabled farmers to irrigate their crops in an otherwise arid land. Yet, this same water has also wrought destruction on the people. The Moslem, Christian and Jewish Prophet, Noah, was allegedly one of the sole survivors of a massive flood caused by the rivers. Today, the rivers still pose a serious threat to Iraq. Only in the last century have the Iraqis developed the means of controlling the rivers in an economically beneficial manner.

There are several dams in Iraq that collect the flood water, store it and allocate it to the farms during the dry season. The dams bolster Iraq's economy by improving the land and the farmers' lives.

Golden fields of wheat at harvest time in northern Iraq.

LAND REFORM

In 1958, the Iraqi government passed a law that prohibited an individual from owning over 1,000 *dunums* of irrigated land or 2,000 *dunums* of rain-watered land. In the 1970s, the amount of land an individual was allowed to own was further decreased. As a result of these changes, rich farmers were forced to divide their large pieces of land. Many individuals bought small parcels of this farmland and formed collective farms with their neighbors. The individual farmer benefited from the collective farms because he or she was able to increase profits while sharing the workload and costs of equipment.

REBUILDING BABYLON

As one of the top oil-producing nations, Iraq has excess money to spend on the restoration of ancient Mesopotamian cities. In 1988, the restoration of the ancient city of Babylon was started.

At one time Babylon was the financial capital of the world. It was ruled by Nebuchadnezzar II who lived in a 700-room palace surrounded by the famous Hanging Gardens of Babylon and a maze of canals. In the center of the ancient city stood the ziggurat of Marduk which the Bible calls the "Tower of Babel."

Babylon straddles the banks of the Euphrates in the central region of the country. The city was built on both sides of the Euphrates with a 33-foot wide bridge connecting the two sides. Babylon was surrounded by a very thick 28-mile long wall. This wall and the famous Hanging Gardens of Babylon were two of the Seven Wonders of the Ancient World.

The ancient city is now being restored. Along with Nebuchadnezzar's palace and the famous brick wall, restorations are being carried out on the Hanging Gardens, the Temple of Hammurabi, the summer palace of the king and the Greek theater.

TRANSPORTATION

Although the overall economy of Iraq was in shambles during the 1980s, the government spent a large share of the domestic budget on improvements to the transportation system. The winding dirt roads linking the major cities became modern express highways in a short period of time. The improved international highways quickly became a lifeline for the transportation of oil.

AIRPORTS Iraq currently has two international airports, one in Baghdad and the other in Basra. The airports service flights to destinations all over the world and the state airline is Iraqi Airways.

The fishing industry thrives along the banks of the Tigris and Euphrates.

The airports are very modern and the one in Baghdad resembles a shrine for Saddam Hussein. Wall-sized murals, statues and photographs of the Iraqi president greet the travelers as they enter and exit the airport.

RAILROADS The railway system of Iraq was very primitive until the 1960s. There was a standard gauge line from Baghdad to the Syrian border and a meter gauge line from Baghdad to Basra. Gauge lines measure the width of the railway lines. The incompatibility of the two lines was a tremendous hindrance in the transportation of cargo. After extensive work and funding from the Soviet Union, Iraq improved its railway system. Today, the system is a standard gauge line that runs from Basra to Baghdad, Mosul, Kirkuk, Syria and Turkey.

IRAQIS

THE PEOPLE OF IRAQ come from diverse ethnic backgrounds and religious affiliations. Approximately 74% of the population are Arabs, 21% Kurds, 3% Turkomans and 1% Persians. The other 1% of the Iraqi people are either Assyrian or Armenian.

Around 54% of the Iraqi people are Shiite ("SHEE-ite") Moslems, 41% are Sunni ("SOON-nee") Moslems, 4% are Christians and the remaining 1% follow another religion such as Judaism. The ancient peoples of Iraq, such as the Babylonians, have assimilated with later immigrants and conquerors.

Throughout the history of Mesopotamia, ethnic and religious rivalries have caused many battles and wars. In present-day Iraq, there is a deep-rooted division between the Arabs and the Kurds. This bitter rivalry is ancient, but was especially fueled in the past century. In the aftermath of the Gulf War in 1991, many Kurds died of starvation or migrated to other countries. Until 1980, there was a substantial percentage of Iranians living in Iraq. During the Iran-Iraq War, some Iranian natives in Iraq were killed while others were driven back to their homeland.

Even the Arab community in Iraq is fragmented along religious lines. The historic conflict between the Shiite and Sunni Moslems continues to escalate and the country is being held together only by the force of Saddam Hussein. Iraqis fear that if Saddam is overthrown, the country will erupt into a bloody holy war between the Shiites and the Sunnis.

Opposite: **Iraqis relax at a local teahouse. About 70% of Iraq's population live in cities and towns.**

Above: **Reed houses such as these have existed in Iraq since the time of the early Sumerians.**

43

Situated at the crossroads between Arabia and Persia, the intermingling of races in Iraq has produced a people of rare beauty.

THE ARABS

Today the majority of Iraqis are Arabs who follow the Moslem faith and speak Arabic. Although the Arabs share Islam and the Arabic language, the people remain increasingly divided on a few important issues. In addition to the deep-rooted religious differences between the Shiites and Sunnis, a wide disparity exists between the different regions of Iraq. The southern areas of Iraq were devastated by bombings during the Iran-Iraq War and the Gulf War. The people of the region blame the central government of Baghdad for their depressed society and resent the lack of monetary support from the wealthier districts.

HISTORY OF THE ARAB PEOPLE The Arab people originated in the Saudi Peninsula, which was separated from the rest of the ancient world by the seas on three sides, the Euphrates on another and by the great expanse of deserts. The Arabs lived in small clans consisting of several families. The clans were constantly raiding each other's villages and warring with each other. The Arabs lived short lives because of their feisty nature. They considered it an honor to die in battle, yet always avenged the deaths of their clan members.

In the 6th century, Mohammed began to convert the Arabs to Islam. The Arabs helped Mohammed spread the word of Islam throughout the present-day countries of Iraq, Syria, Jordan, Saudi Arabia, Morocco and several other nations. As Islam spread, the Arab people migrated to the new lands and drove out the non-believers. In a short time, the Arabs were the primary residents of Iraq and several other countries.

During this period, the Moslems and the Jews fought bitter wars that created intense animosity between the two faiths. This hatred and distrust still exists between the Arabs and the Israelis, who are primarily Jewish.

MODERN ARABS The Iraqi Arabs of today continue in the footsteps of their forefathers. They are strong believers in religion, tradition, culture and family. Iraqi Arabs are a close-knit group who hold the older members of society in the highest regard. Despite their many internal and external conflicts, the Arabs are very a generous, kind people. They are true and supportive friends who form lasting bonds with each other.

Among the Middle Eastern Arabs though, there has been political discord and growing economic differences between the oil-rich countries, such as Kuwait, and poorer Arab nations. The less wealthy Arab countries, including Iraq, are unhappy over the lack of support for economic development and investments in the region, the plight of Palestinians and other Arabs working in the richer states, and the wasting of large sums of money for ostentatious projects such as airports and palaces.

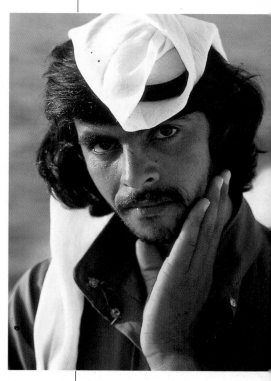

A young Iraqi man, his headcloth messed up by the wind, ponders his country's uncertain future following the disastrous Gulf War.

THE KURDS

The largest non-Arab ethnic group in Iraq are the Kurds. Although a minority in the country, their population is concentrated in the mountains of northern Iraq. The Iraqi Kurds are part of a larger Kurdish "nation" that inhabits northwestern Syria, eastern Turkey and regions of the former Soviet Union. They have a different language and culture, and belong to the minority Sunni sect. The politically-active Kurds hope to eventually secede from their respective countries and form an independent nation.

THE KURDS VERSUS THE ARABS The Iraqi Kurds have desperately fought for independence from Iraq since the 1950s. Under the leadership of Mullah Mustafa Barzani, the Kurds gathered strength and posed a serious threat to the Arabs. They formed groups that launched guerilla attacks on the central government in Baghdad. The attacks were intensified during the Iran-Iraq War.

In 1988, Saddam Hussein retaliated against the Kurds in a violent and tragic way. Iraqi troops flew over Kurdish regions

and dumped poisonous gas on some settlements. Over 5,000 Kurds were killed.

The situation worsened after the Persian Gulf War. When the Iraqi army retreated from Kuwait, it headed north toward Kurdish Country to punish the Kurds for refusing to support Saddam and his army. The Kurds fled into the mountains and escaped to Turkey or Iran. As they fled from the wrath of Saddam, the Republican Guard systematically destroyed the homes and buildings the Kurds left behind.

KURDISH TRIBES The Kurds have traditionally separated into nomadic tribes. In the past few decades, the tribes have become cohesive units organized according to political affiliation. The strongest Kurdish tribes are the Herkki, the Zibari, the Faili and the Sorchi. The Kurdish tribes follow the Islamic faith and almost all of them are Sunni Moslems. The Faili tribe and a few other minor tribes are Shiite Moslems. One group of Kurdish tribes, the Yazidis, are set apart from the rest by their strange religious mix of Christianity, Islam, Zoroastrianism and paganism. The Iraqi Kurds separate themselves from the Yazidis because of their religious disparities.

OTHER MINORITIES

The Turkomans account for approximately 3% of the Iraqi population. These village-dwellers speak a Turkish dialect and reside in northeastern Iraq. The Turkomans migrated in numbers during the 16th century when Iraq became part of the Turkish Ottoman Empire. Although the Turkomans are Sunni Moslems, they tend to disagree about political issues with the Sunni Kurds.

The Assyrians are another minority in Iraq. They are descendants of the Mesopotamians and speak Aramaic. The Assyrians live in the northeastern cities, fall into the middle- to upper-class social bracket, and follow the Christian faith.

SOCIAL SYSTEM

The social system in Iraq is divided into three main tiers: the upper class, the middle class and the lower class. The three class system allows for some upward mobility, but the social status of a person is usually predetermined by birth.

Marsh Arabs use their boats for transportation as well as to fish.

THE UPPER CLASS Members of the upper class in Iraq include government officials, wealthy people with distinguished ancestors, and influential people. But the Iraqi system does not guarantee upper-class standing to the wealthy. In addition to being wealthy, an Iraqi must have a good family name or hold an important position to earn the title of "upper-class citizen."

MIDDLE CLASS Teachers, military personnel, government employees, small landowners and business people, among others, constitute the Iraqi middle class. The people of this social ranking are usually college-educated, moderately wealthy, down-to-earth city dwellers.

LOWER CLASS Iraq's lower class is composed of farmers, rural workers and the unemployed. Iraqis do not place an undesirable stigma on members of the lower class. Although members of this class do not mix with the upper class, there is very little tension between the groups.

COSTUME

The residents of the cities in Iraq dress in styles similar to people in Western countries. Unlike many of the other Arab nations, the women of Iraq are not required to cover their faces with a veil when they are in public. However, rural Iraqis continue dressing in traditional Arab garb.

TRADITIONAL COSTUME FOR WOMEN For centuries the Iraqis have dressed in very traditional costume. The women wore face veils and dark robes called *abaaya,* introduced to Iraq by Arab settlers. The *abaaya* is a long outer cloak which drapes a woman from head to ankle (except for part of her face, which is covered by a veil).

Dressed in the traditional *abaaya*, two rural Iraqi women wait by a desolate and dusty road to catch a bus for the city.

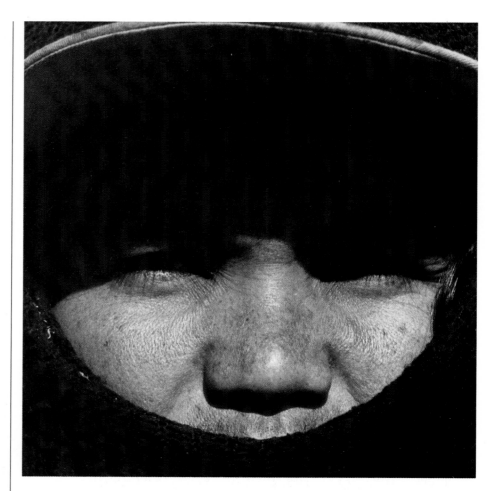

Face veiling had its origin as far back as 1500 B.C. in the Middle East. Besides safeguarding a woman's modesty, it has the practical purpose of protecting a woman's face from the desert sun and windblown sand.

To a foreigner, all Iraqi women may look the same because of this cumbersome costume. However, this is not truly so as Iraqi women do add personal touches to their *abaaya*. For one thing, the cloths used vary in texture and shade. The younger women often add a bright colored fringe or gold threads to their *abaaya*. Wealthier women will belt their costume with a wide, jeweled girdle. Under the *abaaya*, the women wear dresses of beautiful colors.

Iraqi girls used to anticipate the day when they were permitted to don their first veil. The ritual usually occurred when a girl first began her menstrual cycle. The veils were removed only in the home or in the presence of other women.

It was only in the 20th century that Iraqi women began to protest against the Islamic law requiring them to cover their faces. The women in rural towns, on the other hand, find the veil beautiful. These women cannot accept the thought of exposing their faces to men they do not know and are shocked by the audacity of women in the cities who go out in public without the safety of the veil and the *abaaya*.

TRADITIONAL COSTUME FOR MEN The traditional costume for men in Iraq is the caftan, the ankle-length garment with long sleeves. In the past, men wore colorful caftans but today these are plain. In summer, a light cotton caftan is preferred because it is cool. In winter, a warmer woolen one is worn. Baggy pantaloons are worn by Kurdish men. They usually also wear a cummerbund sash.

One of the most distinguishing features of the traditional Iraqi men's costume is the headcloth. Made of cotton or wool it is either worn twisted around the top of the head much like a turban or over the head as a flowing headpiece held in place by a cord. Besides serving as an ornamental piece the headcloth also protects the individual from the burning rays of the sun.

Different forms of head coverings. The turban (*on the right*) is usually worn by rural men.

LIFESTYLE

THE LIFESTYLE OF IRAQIS is determined and molded by their basic values and beliefs. One of the most important values is family loyalty. The family is a cohesive social unit that nurtures its young and old alike. Iraqis also greatly value a person's honor and dignity, and take all risks to maintain an honorable reputation. Central beliefs held by all Iraqis include the ultimate controlling nature of fate, the vast differences between men and women, and the increase of wisdom with age.

Iraqis are generous and loyal people. They are very polite to friends, but not necessarily to strangers. A stranger is not given the same consideration as a friend which causes Iraqis to appear rude to foreigners. Once personal contact is made, however, an Iraqi will change his or her manner very drastically and become very accommodating. But as a friend you are also expected to fulfill certain duties. If a friend asks you for a favor, it is considered very rude to turn him or her down.

Opposite: **The tall reeds in the background provide the Marsh Arabs material for building their houses as well as a means of income. This boy is going to the market to sell his reed mats.**

Below: **Water is difficult to find in the dry and arid regions of western Iraq. Water tankers make regular stops to ensure a dependable water supply for the people who live there.**

In an Iraqi family, women are normally expected to care for the children and the elderly as well as look after the household.

As in any society, there are certain taboos in Iraq. It is considered a disgrace to speak ill of any family member or admit to problems within the family to a non-family member. It is also a taboo for a non-Moslem to enter a mosque or partake in any religious event. Another taboo is to wish bad luck on someone, for it might come true. The upper class consider it a taboo to partake in any manual labor.

FAMILY LIFE

The family is the most important social unit in Iraq. An Iraqi family consists of all related kin, which can include hundreds of people. Most members of the family feel a strong affiliation to their relatives and attempt to maintain a close relationship.

In rural Iraq, families usually live together or nearby each other. The typical household consists of the eldest son, his parents, his wife and his children. Sisters, brothers, cousins, aunts and uncles live in the neighboring homes. The close proximity of the family allows Iraqi children to learn meaningful values and beliefs from their relatives.

In the cities, families do not always live together. Often it is the younger generation who migrate to the cities, leaving the elderly behind. Despite the distance between them, Iraqis are delighted to provide homes or financial support for any relative in need. They know that when they are in trouble other relatives will likewise extend a helping hand.

In a traditional Iraqi family the roles of each member are clearly defined. The children are expected to obey and respect their parents and grandparents. The grandparents offer advice and depend upon their children for their care. The mother serves as the loving and compassionate figure who often spoils the children. The disciplinarian and authoritarian is the father.

The family is placed above everything, including employment. An employer will understand if an employee cannot fulfill his or her job duties because of a family responsibility or emergency.

LINEAGE All members of a family are proud of their lineage. Families on the high end of the social ladder utilize their status to earn high-paying jobs and influential friends. Even lower-class families take extreme pride in their name and prevent their family's reputation from being tarnished.

Many Iraqis have migrated from the rural areas to the cities to work. Here, an itinerant vendor, one of the many rural migrants, ekes out a living selling toys.

Kurdish women love dressing up. Their costumes are rich with intricate embroidery and brilliant colors.

MARRIAGE

The majority of marriages in both rural and urban Iraq are prearranged by the family. The prospective bride or groom usually feels it is best to trust family judgment for the selection of a spouse. Several things are taken into account for marriage, including character, background and financial position. Once two families decide upon a marriage, the bride and groom are allowed to meet each other and become acquainted. If either party is dissatisfied with the match, the marriage will be cancelled.

In traditional Iraqi families and rural areas, marriages preferably occur between first or second cousins. Families choose inter-family marriages because the background and character of the bride and groom are well known. A marriage between cousins also ensures that money and property will remain within the family.

Islamic law states that a man may have up to four wives at one time. Until a few decades ago, before it was outlawed in Iraq, men practiced polygamy, or marriage to more than one person. An older man may have wives whose ages range from his own to that of a girl in her teens.

Marriages in Iraq are based on the ideas of financial security and companionship. Most marriages are successful in these areas. If they are not, divorce is permissible by Islamic law. Both men and women must obtain a divorce through court proceedings, though it is easier for a man to obtain a divorce. An Iraqi man is required to pay his divorced wife enough money to support herself and her children. Both parties are eligible for remarriage without an ugly stigma attached to them. The children of divorced parents normally live with their mother until they are seven to nine years old. At this age they are allowed to choose whom they want to live with.

Due to the shortage of labor, the traditional view that a wife's place is in the home is no longer strictly followed.

The Baghdad Technical College. More woman can be found in schools and universities preparing to pursue careers of their choice. Yet, even among the young and less traditional, the women and men do not mix much.

MEN AND WOMEN

The roles of men and women in Iraqi society have changed in the past few years. Women have been given more freedom than in the past largely because of the eight-year war with Iran and the Gulf War. While Iraqi men were required to join the armed forces and leave their jobs, professions in law, medicine and business became available to women for the first time. Iraqi law approved the status of professional women simply because there were not enough men to fill the vacant positions.

Although women have joined the work force, there are still clearly defined roles for men and women in Iraqi society. Men have complete authority within the family. Women are providers of love and care, but have limited influence in making decisions.

Outside of the home men and women, even husbands and wives, are segregated. When friends get together the sexes usually divide among themselves. It is considered improper for an unmarried man and woman to be alone together. Even men and women who work together avoid sustained contact with the opposite sex. The separation of the sexes is preferred by all because it enables them to feel more comfortable in social settings.

In rural areas, men and women adhere to the traditional sex roles. Women rarely leave the house except to visit friends. It is considered improper for a woman to be seen without her veil or to shop in the market. An unmarried woman's reputation is ruined if she is seen with a man.

Men and women in rural areas are completely segregated. Even married couples rarely spend time together except while sleeping and eating. Men work and spend their leisure time in the company of other men. The women spend their time raising children, cooking, weaving and gossiping with their female friends.

Two gynecologists who represent the new breed of professional women in Iraq. The wars that Iraq has fought have brought many Iraqi women into the work force, filling in positions previously occupied by men.

IRAQI CHILDREN

Children are a very important part of Iraqi society. Iraqi parents love and cherish their children yet raise them with strict discipline. The younger generation is taught, from an early age, the extreme importance of honoring and respecting the elder members of society.

Iraqi children spend the majority of their early years with their mother. She serves as the source of indulgent love and attention. Iraqi children are taught to remain dependent upon their parents until their parents grow too old to support them. Unlike children in the United States, Iraqi children usually live with their parents until they are married. Often, the young adult will choose to continue living with his or her parents even after marriage. If a newly-married couple chooses to live on their own, their parents will help decorate and finance the new home.

In addition to lessons in love and security, Iraqi children learn discipline at an early age as well. Children who misbehave are shamed or punished and forbidden from repeating the action. Parents do not reason with their child or attempt to rationalize their misbehavior.

Iraqi children grow up with their siblings and cousins. The adults in their life include parents, grandparents, aunts and uncles. Because of the cohesive nature of Iraqi families, children learn the strength of the family unit while remaining very close to most relatives.

EDUCATION

The quality of education in Iraq has improved dramatically. Since the 1960s, the number of enrolled students and female students has increased by over 40%.

A six-year elementary school in Iraq is called the primary level. Children between the ages of 6 and 11 attend the primary level of school. Attendance has grown drastically in the past three decades. Almost all Iraqi children attend the primary level.

Adolescents between the ages of 12 and 17 enroll in school at the secondary level. Graduation from the secondary level enables a student to move on to higher education. The first three years of the secondary level focus on the fundamentals of mathematics and science. The remaining three years are similar to the high school curriculum in the United States and prepare students for college.

Vocational schools are technical institutions at the secondary level. During the final three years of the secondary level, students are allowed to choose between college preparatory classes or vocational school. The students in vocational schools learn trade skills in agriculture, industry, home economics and commerce.

Colleges and universities are the highest level of schooling in Iraq. These schools further educate students and enable them to enter the professional job market. According to the constitution, all Iraqi citizens have the right to a free public education up to college level. If a student wishes to further his or her education, an attendance tuition is required. The number of women enrolled in colleges and universities increased dramatically during the 1980s and 1990s.

The Mustansinya campus in Baghdad. There are several public universities in Iraq including four in Baghdad and others in Basra, Mosul, Tikrit, Al-Kufah, Al-Qadisiyah and Al-Anbar. The growing number of institutions enables more young adults in Iraq to pursue higher education.

Modern Baghdad is characterized by elegant avenues and impressive monuments which adorn its streets and squares.

CITY LIFE

As the ancient cradle of civilization, Iraq has been the site of many famous cities. The city has historically played a crucial role in Iraqi society as the center of commerce and government. The cities of Iraq continue this tradition as they experience growth in population and industry.

In the past few decades, there were widespread migrations of Iraqis to urban centers. Entire families have uprooted themselves and relocated to the city. These waves of migration have had an interesting effect. At one time, city residents were a collection of individuals who left home to start a new life in the city. Today, cities are filled with neighborhoods of friends and relatives. This has made the cities a warmer and friendlier place.

During an economic slump in the 1950s, people were forced to build mud homes. The government began to subsidize housing projects which still remain and help to accommodate the growing population. In contrast, the middle- and upper-classes reside in brick apartments or houses surrounded by palm trees and swimming pools.

RURAL LIFE

Many citizens reside in reed and mud huts with their parents and relatives in the small villages and towns of Iraq. Many of the villages consist of several families who collectively form a tribe. The tribe is usually governed by a sheikh and has resident tradesmen and government officials.

The customs of Iraqi villages are deeply-rooted in tradition. The family remains the core of society and parents like to educate their children in a religious-based school. The children believe in following in the footsteps of their parents in choosing a career; for instance, the son of a blacksmith will usually become a blacksmith, too.

Most Iraqi villages lie on the banks of either the Tigris or Euphrates. Water from the rivers is primitively pumped to the villages to irrigate the farms. Agriculture and animal husbandry, the main economic base of the villages, are sustained by river water.

The traditional mud huts of Iraqi villages. In the past few decades, the government has instituted generous programs to assist the villages. Electricity and clean water, among other amenities, are slowly becoming a part of every Iraqi village.

RELIGION

ONE OF THE MOST IMPORTANT ASPECTS of an Iraqi's life is religion. Almost everyone feels strongly about religion. Those people who do not lead a religious life, at least on the surface, are often shunned by their neighbors. Atheists and agnostics are not easily accepted in Iraqi society.

Iraqis try very hard to put their religion into practice in everyday life. Religion is taught in the classroom, dictates marriage and divorce laws, and often plays a part in business and banking. Until the Baath Party took over in the 1960s, the mosque and state were united. Today, the Baath Party recognizes Islam as the official religion, but practices a secularized, or non-religious, form of government.

Several religions are practiced in Iraq. Approximately 95% of the population are Moslems, who belong to one of the two Islamic sects, Shiite or Sunni. Although both Shiites and Sunnis recognize each other as Moslems, the two religions differ in their practice. The Shiites are the predominant Moslem sect in Iraq.

The remaining 5% of the population who are not Moslems are either Christians or Jews. The majority of Christians are Catholic. Despite different religious beliefs, the Iraqi people treat their own and other religions with respect.

Opposite: **Facing the direction of Mecca, a Moslem prays five times daily.**

Below: **The golden dome of the al-Abbas Mosque in Karbala beckons believers from far and wide.**

67

The Imam Hussein Shrine, with its golden domes and minarets, reminds one of the splendor and beauty which characterized the Baghdad caliphate.

RELIGIOUS HISTORY

According to the Bible and the Koran, mankind and religion were born simultaneously in Mesopotamia. The first recorded religion in Mesopotamia was Judaism, written from the time of the Prophet Abraham.

In the beginning, Mesopotamians followed the Jewish faith. With subsequent waves of invasion, new rulers introduced new religions. Many of the Hebrews then fled from Mesopotamia to Israel to escape from persecution when the majority of Mesopotamians were forced to adopt the religious beliefs of the new conquerors. As time progressed, the citizens of Mesopotamia became arch enemies of the Hebrew people. Around 800 B.C., the Assyrians of Mesopotamia began a destructive war that ravaged most of the Middle East including the kingdom of Israel.

Until the coming of Islam, the people of Mesopotamia worshiped many different gods depending on tribal affiliation and family beliefs. The teachings of Mohammed drew the scattered people together under a religion with central beliefs and one god, Allah.

THE SHIITES AND SUNNIS

Visitors to Baghdad by air are always greeted by the gleaming dome of the al-Kadhem Mosque.

After the death of the Prophet Mohammed, the Moslems were split over conflicting views of the role of the caliph. This differing view created a chasm that exists today.

The Shiites took the firm stance that the caliphate should be held by descendants of Mohammed believing them to possess the capability for spiritual leadership and the ability to interpret the many mysteries of the Koran. The Sunnis, on the other hand, believed that the caliph should be elected by the people.

Despite similar beliefs about the teachings of Mohammed and the Koran, the two sects of Islam increasingly have grown apart. The Shiites feel that the Sunnis, the minority sect in Iraq which holds political power, have subjected the Shiites to unfair discrimination. The Sunnis fear that the Shiites will forcefully drive them into exile. Unfortunately, the chasm between the sects has not improved despite attempts at reconciliation by the Baath Party. This rivalry seems to be on the verge of erupting into civil war.

69

ISLAM IN IRAQ

In order to understand Iraqi culture it is crucial to study the religion of Islam. Most people assume that the religion began in 7th century Arabia when the Prophet Mohammed preached and spread the faith. A Moslem, however, will contend that Islam was born with God, whom they refer to as Allah. Moslems believe that Allah created the world and the first man, Adam. Adam's descendant, Ishmael, went to Mecca and his descendants grew up as Moslems in present-day Saudi Arabia.

Islam was taught and spread through the Prophet Mohammed. He was born in approximately A.D. 571 at a time of unrest. There was much fighting and killing. The kind and benevolent Mohammed removed himself from society because he was unhappy with all of the evil. When he reached adulthood, the voice of Allah called out to him, urging him to, "Cry in the name of thy Lord." Mohammed told his wife of his experience and she became his first convert. The years passed and though he faced opposition,

The minaret, from which the muezzin calls all believers to prayer, is a common architectural feature to all mosques.

Mohammed converted thousands of people to Islam. He died with almost all of Arabia under his influence, including the country of Iraq.

The Islamic faith is based on strict principles called the Five Pillars of Islam. The first pillar is a creed that states: "There is no God but Allah, and Mohammed is his Prophet." The second pillar emphasizes constancy in prayer. A Moslem must pray facing the holy town of Mecca five times daily. Charity, or giving to those less fortunate, is the third pillar. The fourth pillar is the observance of the holy month, Ramadan. During this holy month, Moslems must fast and go without any food or drink during the day. They must also avoid war or long journeys. The final pillar of Islam is the hajj, the pilgrimage to Mecca. During his or her lifetime, every Moslem must journey once to the holy city of Mecca and visit the site where Allah first spoke to Mohammed.

Islam's Bible is called the Koran and is believed to have been dictated by Allah himself. The Koran is widely read and memorized. It teaches about the four major issues of the Islamic faith: Allah, Creation, Man, and the Day of Judgment. Moslems believe strongly in the afterlife and the continuation of life.

The Moslems of Iraq gather for worship in mosques; however, they are free to pray anywhere they choose. Friday is set aside as the holy day and at noon, Moslems worship Allah and give alms to the poor. Many businesses and stores are closed on Fridays in observance of this sacred day.

JOURNEY TO MECCA

One of the five pillars of Islam states that each Moslem must make a journey to Mecca once in his or her lifetime. Mecca is a sacred city located in Saudi Arabia. Six miles from Mecca, the pilgrims prepare to enter the shrine. They bathe in a special liquid and don specific clothes. The men and the women separate into groups of the same sex and remain apart until the journey is completed.

When the pilgrims arrive in the city, they perform 10 rites in the following order:

1. Enter the Gate of Peace
2. Kiss the black stone of the Ka'bah (a cube-shaped monument in the Grand Mosque of the city)
3. Circle the Ka'bah seven times and touch the stone each time around
4. Pray at the tomb of Abraham
5. Ascend to the tops of Mount Safa and Mount Marwah and then run between them seven times
6. Journey to Mount Arafat
7. Listen to the sermon on Mount Arafat
8. Celebrate in Muzdalifah, a city between Mecca and Arafat
9. "Stone the Devils" using specific pebbles to throw at the pillars in Mina
10. Visit the tomb of Mohammed

After the 10 rites are performed, the journey to Mecca is complete and the pilgrims return to their homeland.

Opposite: *Surahs* from the Koran. The Koran is divided into 114 chapters, known as *Surahs*. Written in half prose and half poetry, they contain language of great power and beauty, especially when read out aloud.

CHRISTIANITY

Although the majority of people in Iraq follow the Islamic religion, a large number of Iraqis practice Christianity and a small number are Jewish. Ever since the beginning of recorded history, Moslems and Jews have argued and fought in holy wars. Therefore, most Jews prefer to live apart from the Moslems. Many Jews in Iraq returned to Israel when the Jewish state was formed in 1948.

Christians, however, continue to reside in Iraq and practice their religion as their Western counterparts. Like Moslems and Jews, Christians believe in one god. Their Messiah, or Prophet, is Jesus Christ and their holy book is the Bible.

Iraq is the setting of many biblical stories including the creation of man. The Garden of Eden, the home of the biblical Adam and Eve, is believed to be in Iraq. In the Garden of Eden, Eve took a bite of the forbidden fruit and committed mankind's first sin against God. Abraham, patriarch of the Jews and Christians, was born in Ur, an ancient city in southern Iraq. Another biblical story set in Iraq is the story of Daniel who was thrown in the furnace of King Nebuchadnezzar's palace in Babylon and was unharmed because he was a believer in God.

The Christians in Iraq worship in churches and usually follow the Catholic faith. Sunday is the universal Christian holy day in which all believers attend Mass to worship and give alms. Sunday is a day of rest and, therefore, all Christian businesses and shops in Iraq are closed on this holy day.

THE KORAN AND THE BIBLE

Among the major religions of the world, Islam, Christianity and Judaism are closely related. Although there are distinct differences among the three religions, there are notable similarities as well. Christianity and Judaism share the teachings of the Old Testament of the Bible. Even more similar are Islam and Christianity which share common beliefs of both the Old and New Testaments of the Bible. Similarities between the Islamic Koran and the Christian Bible include:

- the belief in both Heaven and Hell
- the importance of faith in God, or Allah
- the Day of Judgment
- Satan, or the Devil
- the story of the Creation of mankind: the first man, Adam, and the first woman, Eve
- prophets such as Adam, Noah, Abraham, Moses and Jesus
- the belief that the Virgin Mary gave birth to Jesus
- the belief that Jesus was able to perform miracles

The Moslems believe that their religion is a continuation of Christianity and Judaism into the completion of one true faith. Any Moslem, including one in Iraq, would be disappointed by the Christian and Jewish people of the West who dismiss the Islamic faith as completely foreign to their own. When the Koran and the Bible are closely examined, it is easy to observe the basic core upon which Islam, Christianity and Judaism are built.

LANGUAGE

THE DOMINANT LANGUAGE in Iraq is Arabic. Approximately 76% of the population speak Arabic. It is the official language of Iraq, the Middle Eastern Arab nations and the Islamic religion. Arabic is a member of the Semitic family of languages and is related to Hebrew and Syriac.

The remainder of the people in Iraq speak some Arabic although their mother tongue is another language. The other languages of Iraq include Kurdish, Turkic, Armenian and Persian.

Kurdish is spoken by the Kurds in the northern region. The language is part of the Iranian branch of the Indo-European family. It is written in Roman script and spoken by approximately 10 million people in Iraq, Turkey, Iran, Syria and Armenia, part of the former Soviet Union.

The Moslem Turkomans are a minority group in Iraq who speak a Turkish dialect that is related to the languages of Central Asia and even Mongolia.

Armenian is a minor language in Iraq although it is spoken by over four million people in Iraq, Lebanon, Syria, Iran, Turkey and the former Soviet Union. It was developed in A.D. 400 by the missionary Mesrop Mashtots. It consists of 38 letters and is in the Indo-European language family.

A small percentage of Iraqis speak Persian, the official language of Iran. Persian contains many Arabic words and is written in Arabic. It is a member of the Indo-European family along with Arabic and Armenian.

Opposite: **Street signs in Baghdad, in Arabic and English.**

Below: **Cuneiform, or wedge-shaped writing, is the earliest evidence of a written language. The Sumerians formed these figures by imprinting them on wet clay.**

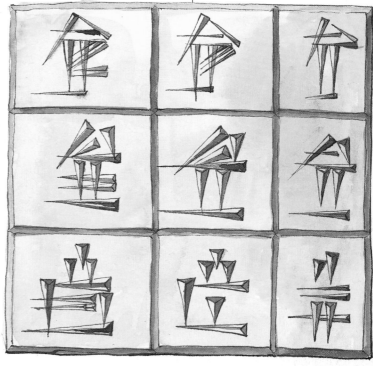

77

A title page of the Koran is rendered in beautiful Arabic script.

Written Arabic has not existed nearly as long as the language itself. The Arabs did not trust the written word and relied on the oral tradition for communication. After the advent of Islam, the Arabs produced a beautiful script that committed their language to writing. The Arabic script is an exquisite form of calligraphy that transforms ordinary writing into an art form. The Koran, the holy book of Islam, was copied thousands of times in the beautiful calligraphy of Arabic. These copies of the Koran help scholars trace the development of written Arabic.

ARABIC

Arabic is one of the world's major languages and is the sixth official language of the United Nations. It is also the sacred tongue of the Moslems. Arabic originated in Saudi Arabia around A.D. 600. The Moslem Prophet Mohammed began to preach his beliefs in Arabic, and the language quickly spread to the near East, Persia, Egypt and North Africa.

Arabic consists of three different tongues: classical Arabic, colloquial Arabic and modern standard Arabic. Classical Arabic is the language of the Islamic Koran. Colloquial Arabic varies from region to region. In Iraq, the colloquial tongue is called Iraqi Arabic. Each area has its own version of spoken Arabic and it is often difficult to understand someone from another region speaking in his or her own local tongue. Modern standard Arabic is the official written language of Iraq and the other Arab countries.

An Iraqi woman reads a magazine which is published in Arabic, the official language of Iraq.

Arabic has an alphabet of 29 letters with 26 consonants and three vowels. Arabic is written from right to left and there is no difference between capital and small letters. When spoken, Arabic sounds both rich and guttural. In general, Arabic is a very difficult language to learn and master because of its differences with the other major languages of the world.

Some Arab words may not be as foreign as they sound. Through the centuries, trade between Europe and the Middle East has resulted in the adoption of Arabic words in the English language. Some words which we commonly use are: cotton, giraffe, lime, mummy, sherbet, sofa and sugar.

BODY LANGUAGE

A very important part of communication in Iraq is the use of gestures and nonverbal communication. While speaking, an Iraqi uses his or her eyes and hands to emphasize a point. Usually Iraqi women do not use gestures as often as the men. Some of the universal Arab gestures are as follows:

1. Raised eyebrows and tilted-back head means "No."
2. Clicking sounds made with the tongue mean "No."
3. Right hand on the heart after shaking hands is a sign of sincerity.
4. A fist with an extended thumb is a sign of victory.
5. Right hand moving up and down with the palm facing down means "Be quiet."
6. Right forefinger moving right to left means "No."
7. Right hand moving away from the body with palm facing down means "Go away."
8. Right hand out while opening and closing the hand means "Come here."

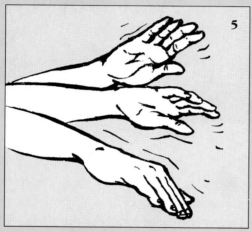

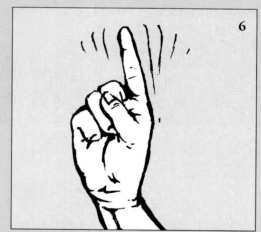

In Iraqi society, body language thus plays an integral role in communication. While speaking with another person, Iraqis touch each other more often than Westerners and stand closer together. People of the same sex will often hold hands while talking to each other even if they are virtual strangers.

Iraqis are very enthusiastic when they greet each other. A kiss on the cheek or an embrace are the standard greetings between members of the same sex. Members of the opposite sex verbally greet each other but have no physical contact. Even married couples refrain from a public display of affection when they are greeting each other.

A vast amount of Islamic literature is sold in the streets and in little book-shops.

CONVERSATIONS

After greeting each other, men and women usually separate into two or more groups of the same sex. It is not common for men and women who are not well acquainted to converse with one another. The Western tradition of men and women gathering in public places to mingle with members of the opposite sex rarely occurs in Iraq.

In conversation, Iraqis ask personal questions that delve into one's marriage, children and salary. Although a foreigner is often displeased by such questions, Iraqis are often offended if they are not asked by their friends. Iraqis talk a lot and repeat important information during a conversation. They do not hesitate to interrupt nor are they offended when someone speaks over their own conversation. An Iraqi conversation consisting of more than two people is usually loud, emotional and filled with gestures.

NAMES

Iraqis have long names that include their first name, their father's name, their paternal grandfather's name and a family name. In Iraqi society, a person is immediately called by their first name which is sometimes preceded by Mr., Mrs., Dr., or Miss. Parents are often politely addressed by their eldest son's name preceded by "Umm" for the mother and "Abu" for the father. Thus, the parents of a son named Abdi would be called "Umm Abdi" and "Abu Abdi."

When an Iraqi woman marries, she does not legally adopt her husband's name. Instead, a married woman retains her mother's family name as an honorable tribute to her family.

Names often indicate not only family, but religion and country of origin as well. A Western name will invariably belong to a Christian while names beginning with "Abdel" or containing "deen" belong to a Moslem.

Men will often have the same first and third name because they are named after their paternal grandfather. The equivalent of this pattern in English would be someone named Thomas John Thomas Jones. When a person's name becomes too long, a few of the names will be dropped. As a rule, the father's name and the family name will be retained but the others can be dropped. Because of this practice children of the same family will often have different names or a different combination of names.

The Kurds of Iraq, though Moslems, perceive themselves as being different from other Iraqis as their mother tonque is Kurdish and not Arabic.

ARTS

IRAQ IS A COUNTRY with an extensive artistic history. As the site of the world's first civilization, Iraq has produced great literature, beautiful artifacts, magnificent carpets and unique architectural styles. As Iraqi archeologists continue to excavate the ruins of ancient Mesopotamian cities, more exciting historical discoveries are being uncovered each year.

Storytelling has played an important part in Iraqi culture since the beginning of time. These stories have contributed to Middle Eastern and Western literature and art throughout history. One piece of literature that was strongly influenced by Mesopotamian stories and songs is the Bible. The stories of the Garden of Eden, the Song of Solomon and the Book of Psalms, among others, were influenced by the culture of Mesopotamia. Many of the Greek epic poems and myths, such as *The Iliad* and *Aesop's Fables,* are elaborate editions of Mesopotamian stories.

Iraq's most famous pieces of literature are the *Epic of Gilgamesh* and *The Thousand and One Nights.* The first piece of literature is an Akkadian epic poem that describes the ruler of Erech, Gilgamesh, who fought to attain immortality. *The Thousand and One Nights* is an entertaining collection of thrilling stories of brave journeys, romance and adventure.

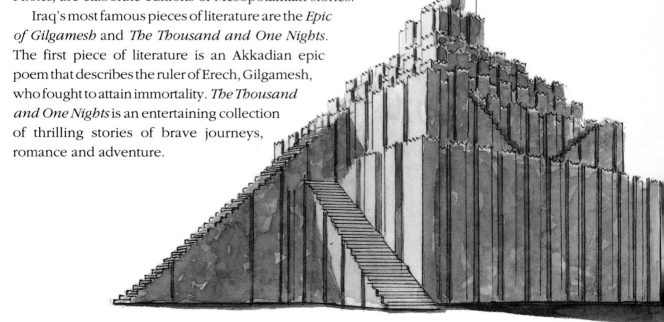

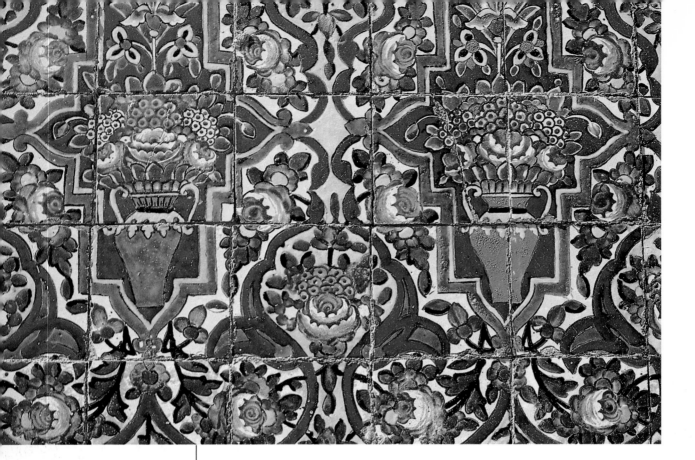

The clean simple lines of Islamic architecture are often adorned with intricate designs and filled with a dazzling array of colors on hand-painted tiles and ceramics.

ISLAMIC ART

Islamic art forbids the artist from portraying any human or animal forms. Therefore, the majority of Islamic art depicts imaginative creatures and intricate designs. Many pieces of Islamic art contain inscriptions from the Koran and beautiful Arabic script adorns most of the pieces.

Islamic pottery is very colorful and ornate. The materials used in the production of pots range from bronze to earthenware. In ancient Islamic art, the use of gold and silver was strictly forbidden by the Prophet Mohammed.

One of the most magnificent artifacts in Islamic art is the carpet. Carpets are woven from fine threads in magnificent colors and are the object of many stories in Iraqi culture.

EARLY ISLAMIC ART The Moslem conquerors spread the preachings of Mohammed during the seventh and eighth centuries. The conquerors overthrew the Sasanid dynasty and inherited the state treasury and institutions. New-found wealth and prestige led to artistic endeavors.

Works of architecture were commissioned. The wealthy Mesopotamians hired artists to weave beautiful carpets of special design for the family. In the middle of the eighth century, pottery and the textile industry became popular in the Islamic art circle as increasingly more wealthy families hired artists.

ISLAMIC PATRONAGE The majority of the Islamic art was commissioned by patrons or wealthy citizens and royalty. Talented artists were hired to create an artifact that was innovative, elaborate and one of its kind. This patronage encouraged the artists to develop exciting new modes of artistic expression. At the same time, it created a plethora of Islamic art in Mesopotamia that, through the centuries, people have been able to enjoy. Some of the commissioned artifacts included glass goblets or bowls decorated with elaborate designs in bright colors. One of the favorite colors of the Islamic artists was "Mohammed blue," a color developed by the Chinese.

As a patron's art collection grew, he or she often commissioned the building of a special museum to house the valuable artifacts. The citizens of the community were extended invitations to these museums where the artwork was displayed. Several generous patrons have given these private museums to the city or to Moslem institutions for the benefit of the community.

Islamic art, which frowns upon the depiction of images, has transformed Arabic calligraphy into an art form. Wall decorations containing verses from the Koran are commonly found in many Moslem homes.

IRAQI LITERATURE

Early Iraqi literature originated as stories passed down from one generation to the next. Eventually this oral literature, such as *The Thousand and One Nights,* was recorded. Historians believe that Mesopotamia was the first civilization to experiment with writing. Clay tablets and artwork dating from the Sumerian age reflect a written form of communication, though much of the literature for centuries remained oral. Today, Iraqis continue to enjoy literature through the art of storytelling.

Iraqi literature experienced a renaissance, or rebirth, when, after centuries of intellectual and cultural decay following the end of the Abbasid caliphate, many brilliant works were written in the 1950s. In addition to the great increase in volume, the literature reflected a changing style. The epic stories were replaced by short stories filled with the struggles and experiences of everyday life. Poetry also developed into the non-rhyming, personalized form already popular in the Western world.

IRAQ'S MOST POPULAR BOOK The most popular and well-read book in Iraq is the Koran. Although the Koran was not written in Iraq, it is a reflection of the Iraqis' religious beliefs and principles. The Koran is a written record of the teachings of the Prophet Mohammed. The Iraqis read, memorize and live by the teachings of the Koran.

Opposite: **Copper and brass objects are still worked by hand using traditional methods.**

Below: **A fountain sculpture recreates an episode from that delightful story,** *Ali Baba and the Forty Thieves.*

Simple folk art with nature motifs cater to a small but growing tourist industry.

CRAFTS

Making handcrafted items is very popular in Iraq. Each year, hundreds of art fairs are scheduled to accommodate the production of the country's artists. Many of the crafts made in Iraq are sold, but the majority are produced at home for household use. The principal crafts designed by Iraqis are jewelry, rugs, blankets, leather and pottery.

Craft-making is one of the favorite leisure activities of women in the smaller villages and towns of Iraq. During the afternoons, the women gather together to make useful and beautiful household items. Remarkable rugs and blankets of startling colors are handwoven by the women and their children. Several households will share ownership of a pottery wheel which the women use to make jugs, bowls and ornamental objects.

VISUAL ARTS

Television, film, painting and sculpture are the predominant visual arts of Iraq. The popularity of television and film in Iraqi culture has greatly increased during the past few years while painting and sculpture are traditional Iraqi arts. The majority of the paintings are housed in museums or homes in Iraqi cities. Many sculptures, however, adorn the streets, corners, gardens and plazas of Iraq. Under the Baath regime, paintings and statues of Saddam Hussein have appeared all over the country. When Iraq invaded Kuwait in 1990, many of the statues and paintings of Saddam were transported to Kuwait to remind the citizens of their new leader.

ARCHEOLOGICAL DIGS

Due to its ancient history, Iraq is an archeologist's dream. For centuries, archeological excavations have been carried out at thousands of sites in Iraq. Hidden cities, preserved artifacts and other traces of old civilizations have been uncovered.

ANCIENT HEALING CENTER In 1990, a team of archeologists uncovered a temple in the ancient city of Nippur. The temple was dedicated to Gula, the Babylonian goddess of healing. The dedication to a goddess affiliated with medicine indicates that the temple served as an ancient hospital or healing center. Within the temple, the archeologists discovered ancient artifacts such as a bronze dog figurine with an inscription to the goddess Gula. Many of the other artifacts found in the temple were statues of humans holding their stomachs, throats or backs in the guise of physical pain.

The existence of the temple enables modern Iraqis to learn about their predecessors. Archeologists believe that the inhabitants of Nippur and the surrounding Mesopotamian cities entered the temple for medical treatment. The presence of tablets and statues with inscriptions allows historians to study the ancient practice of medicine, the use of herbs and plants, and the roles of doctors and magicians.

THE EXCAVATION OF MASHKAN-SHAPIR Archeologists were thrilled to discover the ancient city of Mashkan-Shapir in early 1989. Historians believe that Mashkan-Shapir was a major Mesopotamian city in approximately 2000 B.C. The ruins of the city are located between the Tigris and Euphrates in the southern Iraqi desert.

Mashkan-Shapir, one of the world's oldest cities, was destroyed in approximately 1720 B.C. and was never reoccupied. The city was surrounded by a thick wall with hidden gates. Along the wall, the residents of Mashkan-Shapir left behind clay tablets and cylinders. While studying the tablets and cylinders, archeologists detected traces of Sumerian cuneiform ("KYU-nee-a-form"), a form of writing in Mesopotamia. Many of the tablets were dedicated to Nergal, the ancient Babylonian god of death and archeologists believe that this indicates that Mashkan-Shapir was the city of Nergal.

Within the city walls, archeologists discovered the remains of a cemetery, palace and a place of worship. The discovery of employee's recorded hours on the city's walls and clay tablets teaches historians about the work ethics and lifestyle of Mesopotamians.

Elaborate canals, streets and neighborhoods suggest an advanced city government and planning committee. In all, the discovery of this ancient city has allowed archeologists, historians and citizens of Iraq to understand the complex social and artistic history of Mesopotamia.

GOVERNMENT CENSORSHIP AND CONTROL OF THE ARTS

The Baath regime has introduced the citizens of Iraq to several previously unknown luxuries including modern health care, advanced technology and improved education. Several art museums, such as the Saddam Hussein Art Center (above), can be found in Baghdad and other cities. Along with these benefits to society, the Baath regime has instituted severe punishments for those who choose to disobey its harsh and dictatorial rule.

The regime exercises strict control over the arts and there is government censorship of books, films and newspapers. Foreign journalists reporting in Iraq are closely watched by government officials. If a journalist discovers something the Iraqi government is trying to hide, their broadcast is either censored or the journalist is punished. Iraqi journalists are similarly treated for the anti-government publications despite the constitutional right of free speech.

Literature and films have been equally censored under the Baathists. Artists cleverly avoid any negative reflections on the government or Saddam Hussein. It is an artistic tragedy that literature and films are censored, and this has curtailed the publication efforts of many citizens. An author in Iraq today usually prefers to sacrifice artistic integrity rather than risk punishment by the Iraqi government.

More than 38 feet high, the famous Ishtar Gate leading to the city of Babylon was decorated with glazed brick reliefs of animals. The walls were so solid, they survived the destruction rained upon them by Persian troops in 600 B.C.

IRAQI ARCHITECTURE

The architecture of Iraq is varied according to location, intended use of the building and the time of construction. Iraqi cities such as Baghdad possess a modern architectural style in some areas of the city while other areas retain the charm of Iraq's past. Ultra-modern high rise apartment complexes and business offices have been built in Baghdad. The advanced technology of the country in the past few decades has enabled architects to design elaborate buildings that compete with the modern structures of the West. Unlike the big cities, the small Iraqi villages and towns have a relatively primitive, bland and unattractive architecture.

RELIGIOUS SHRINES

The architectural design of Moslem shrines in Iraq is amazingly beautiful. Holy shrines are located everywhere, from the big cities to the small towns of Iraq. Each shrine differs slightly in architectural style, but they all resemble the Shiite mosque in Baghdad.

The shrines are surrounded by a wall topped with exquisitely carved golden domes and minarets. The wall encloses the shrine and a magnificent courtyard. The shrine itself is covered with detailed mosaics in bright colors. Great pillars that rise to a high, arched entrance support the shrines. Above the entrance are hundreds of mirrors arranged to reflect the sunlight.

These beautiful shrines are scattered throughout Iraq. Even primitive and unattractive small towns possess these magnificent religious structures.

An uncommon sight today is this old mud house, which with its shuttered windows and screens provided both privacy and ventilation.

LEISURE

THE DIFFERENT REGIONS OF IRAQ permit their citizens to participate in a variety of leisure activities. In the north people use the steep mountains and cooler climate for outdoor activities such as hiking and camping. Residents of the regions surrounding the Tigris and Euphrates enjoy fishing and swimming during the summer months. City dwellers have the opportunity to visit exquisite art museums, bountiful bazaars and large shopping complexes. All regions of Iraq share an interest in the country's favorite sport of soccer.

Opposite: **Friday picnic in a park in southern Iraq by the Shatt al-Arab.**

Left: **A teahouse in Mosul, northern Iraq, is filled with men. Iraqi women are expected to remain at home and are seldom seen in such public places.**

One of the most famous characters of Shahrazad's stories is Sindbad the Sailor, the wealthy explorer who experienced thrilling adventures in his seven journeys around the world.

COMPANIONSHIP

Visiting friends and relatives is a favorite leisure activity for all Iraqis. Most people set aside time every day or once a week to visit each other. Children and teenagers spend their time together playing sports and games and watching television. Young Iraqis frequent elegant restaurants and dancing or drinking establishments with their friends and relatives. Older Iraqis spend time with their peers talking and telling stories. Regardless of the activity Iraqis choose, they place great importance in spending their free time with friends and relatives.

STORYTELLING

Iraqis love to tell stories. They tell tales of fortune, luck, sorrow and religious significance. The most popular story in Iraq and many other countries is *The Thousand and One Nights*. There is no definitive author of the story, rather it is a collection of several storytellers through the centuries. The tale was first told in Mesopotamia during the reign of Caliph Harun al-Rashid.

The tale begins with a king who distrusted and hated all women. This king, Sultan Shahryar, married a new wife every day and had her slain the next morning. This hateful practice continued for years until the only eligible bride left for Sultan Shahryar was the daughter of the vizier, Shahrazad. Shahrazad agreed to marry the king in an attempt to stop the daily murders of innocent women.

Before Sultan Shahryar fell asleep the first night, Shahrazad told him an exciting story and stopped just

SINDBAD THE SAILOR'S SEVEN JOURNEYS

1. On his first journey, Sindbad left his home city of Baghdad in search of adventure and wealth. His ship landed on a beautiful island that resembled Paradise, but turned out to be a dormant fish. When the fish woke, all of the men except Sindbad escaped on the ship. While his crew presumed him dead, Sindbad lived on an island with a king until he was able to return to his home.

2. On his second journey, Sindbad was deserted on an island with giant birds, poisonous serpents and magnificent diamonds. Sindbad bravely escaped the perilous land and became a wealthy man with the sale of the diamonds.

3. On his third journey, Sindbad met with vicious apes, an angry giant, a female ogre and a deadly serpent. Once again, Sindbad escaped unharmed, found precious goods and returned to Baghdad an even richer man.

4. Sindbad's fourth journey brought him to the island of the Magis and their king. Visitors to this mysterious island were fed excessive amounts of food until they became very fat. When the men reached a certain weight, the king roasted and ate them. Sindbad left the island, found jewels on another and then returned home.

5. On his fifth journey, Sindbad the sailor discovered an island of gigantic and sumptuous pumpkins, with citizens that pelted apes with pebbles. After spending time in this strange land, Sindbad took some coconuts and returned to Baghdad.

6. During his sixth journey, Sindbad once again was the victim of a shipwreck. He landed on a beautiful island with magnificent lakes and rugged mountains. The island, called Sarandib, was ruled by a generous king who gave Sindbad a position of honor. Eventually Sindbad missed his homeland and returned to Baghdad.

7. Sindbad's final journey took him back to Sarandib bearing gifts for the king. On the passage home, Sindbad's ship was captured by demons and Sindbad was sold as a slave. As a slave, Sindbad discovered a valley of elephant tusks, sold the tusks for his freedom and returned to Baghdad to stay.

before the climax. He was so anxious to discover the outcome of the story that he did not kill his new bride. Every night for years, Shahrazad told the king a story before he fell asleep. Her exciting tales of adventure, love, fortune, princes, kings and queens are the stories that collectively with others became known as *The Thousand and One Nights* or *The Arabian Nights' Entertainment*.

Opposite: **The calm and peaceful waters of the Shatt al-Arab are ideal for swimming, fishing and sailing.**

SPORTS

In the past few decades Iraqis have become very involved in sports. The country's favorite sport is soccer, but there is also a growing interest in boating, basketball, volleyball and boxing. Iraq's recent political turmoil has prevented many sportsmen and women from doing well on the international sports scene.

SOCCER The most popular sport in the world is also the favorite sport of the Iraqi people. In the United States this sport is called soccer, but to the rest of the world, it is known as football. Soccer's popularity has grown tremendously in the middle to late 20th century. In 1986, Iraqi soccer finally achieved world recognition when its team was invited to attend the World Cup as the Asian representative. The World Cup, sponsored by FIFA, the Federation Internationale de Football Association, is held every four years.

Iraq is a member of the Asian Football Confederation (AFC) which was founded in 1954. The country participates every year in the Asian Nations Cup, a competition for all members of the AFC. Although soccer has been played for less than half a century in Iraq, the sport is thriving. The games in Baghdad draw thousands of boisterous and supportive fans. The Iraqi soccer teams are very encouraged by their country's support of the sport and are confident that they will continue to do well internationally.

OTHER SPORTS IN IRAQ In addition to soccer and national competition sports such as basketball, volleyball and boxing, the Iraqis enjoy swimming and boating on the Tigris and Euphrates or in the Persian Gulf. The warmer temperatures in the southern regions of Iraq allow Iraqis to enjoy water sports for most of the year.

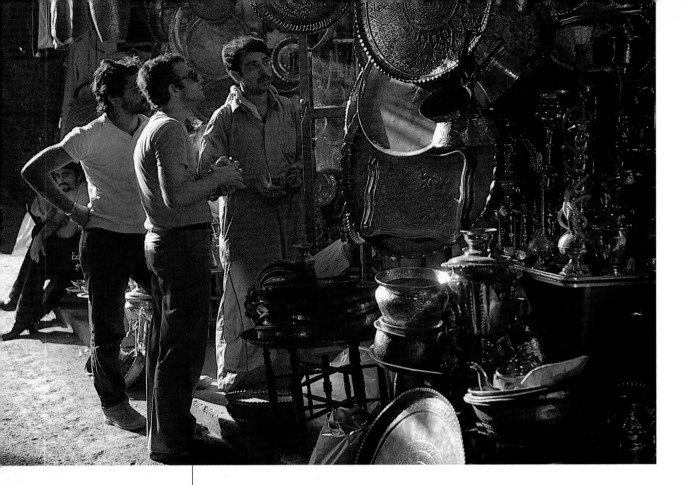

There is no better place to shop for brass- and copperware than in the tiny and crowded shops lining a bazaar.

BAZAARS AND MUSEUMS

Baghdad is famous for its bazaars. Although most cities and villages in Iraq have bazaars, Baghdad's are the largest and have the widest selection. A visitor to a bazaar is surrounded by throngs of people scurrying in search of the finest fruit or the best deal. The bazaars offer a sumptuous array of fruit, fresh meat and exotic spices. They attract Iraqis from all socioeconomic groups although the women of wealthy families usually send someone to shop for them. The prices of items at the bazaars are usually determined through a heated bargaining process between the buyer and the seller.

As the cradle of ancient civilization, Iraq possesses some of the finest antique pieces of art. Items found in the archeological digs of Mesopotamia are displayed in some of the art museums in Iraq. Exquisite jewels, elaborate thrones, and fancy combs from the many caliphs, kings, and rulers of Iraq are displayed.

RURAL ACTIVITIES

Unlike the city-dwellers of Iraq, the residents of the small villages and towns scattered around the country live a relatively simple life steeped in tradition. The men and the women remain separate for the most part and leisure activities exist predominantly between members of the same sex.

Marsh Arab children are allowed to own canoes at a very young age.

ACTIVITIES FOR MEN Men enjoy spending their leisure time hunting and fishing with their friends. Most rural towns are located along one of the twin-rivers where the wildlife and fish are abundant. Thus it is possible to supply one's family with food after a day of hunting or fishing. These trips are exciting and young boys eagerly await the day when their fathers will take them on a hunting expedition.

The men are usually responsible for going to the markets and bazaars to buy food. On market days, groups of friends will spend the day together while leisurely shopping for food and drinks.

ACTIVITIES FOR WOMEN Women in small villages and towns visit each other almost every day. While their husbands are working or playing, the women gather together to talk, cook or make handicrafts. The women also take care of and plan interesting activities for the children who are not yet in school.

FESTIVALS

FESTIVALS IN IRAQ are often joyous occasions with families and friends gathered together for feasts and merriment. Many of these occasions celebrate secular events such as marriage, birth and independence. The majority of festivals in Iraq, however, have religious significance.

Some of these religious holidays are solemn, observed by fasting, prayers, storytelling, and processions. Dates of the Moslem festivals and holidays are determined by the Moslem lunar calendar rather than the standard calendar. Therefore, these special days occur at a different time each year.

According to Moslem tradition, Friday is the official day of rest. Most of the business offices and all government institutions are closed every Friday. The only businesses that remain open are managed by Christians or non-Moslems. Christians observe Sunday as their day of rest and attend church.

Opposite: **A folkloric dance troupe performs an item. In Iraq, folk music and dances often accompany the celebration of important events.**

HOLIDAYS IN IRAQ

MOSLEM HOLIDAYS

Month 1, days 1-10	Muharram
Month 1, day 1	The Tree at the Boundary
Month 1, days 1-9	Oh, Hussein! Oh, Hussein!
Month 1, day 10	Ashura
Month 3, day 11	Maulid an-Nabi (Mohammed's birthday)
Month 9	Ramadan
Month 9, last day	Eid al-Fitr
Month 12, day 10	Eid al-Adha

NATIONAL HOLIDAYS

April 28	Birthday of Saddam Hussein
July 14	Anniversary of the revolution (overthrow of the government by the Baath Party)
October 13	Independence from the British Mandate

CHRISTIAN FESTIVALS

April (specific Sunday)	Easter
December 25	Christmas

Shiite Moslem pilgrims visit and embrace the shrine of al-Hussein during Muharram. Moslems believe Hussein was a martyr who chose to die so all believers could enter Paradise upon death.

MUHARRAM

The New Year is celebrated during the first month of the Moslem calendar year. During Muharram, Moslems honor the martyr Hussein, discuss the Tree at the Boundary and celebrate the landing of Noah's Ark.

OH, HUSSEIN! OH, HUSSEIN! Muharram honors Hussein, the grandson of the Prophet Mohammed, who was killed in battle by an enemy. On the first nine days of Muharram, the story of Hussein is recounted nightly. As the believers listen to the highly emotional story, they will often begin crying and shout, "Oh, Hussein! Oh, Hussein!"

Other events commemorate the death of Hussein. The people re-enact the marriage of Hussein's daughter and the burial of Hussein. One of the most intriguing events of Muharram is the sight of Shiite Moslem men chained together and parading through the streets beating themselves and each other with chains, belts and sticks. Shiite Moslems inflict physical pain on themselves to imitate the sufferings of Hussein.

An illustration of Noah's Ark and two of every living creature, one male and one female, making their way into the ark, which would protect them through the great flood.

THE TREE AT THE BOUNDARY During the week of Muharram, Moslems tell the story of the Tree at the Boundary. According to legend, on the first night of Muharram, an angel shakes a tree at the boundary of Paradise and earth. Each leaf on the tree represents a living person. If a leaf falls while the angel shakes the tree, the person whose name appears on the leaf will die in the coming year. The people do not know which leaves fall off the tree until someone dies during the year. When someone dies, the Moslems are confident that his or her name was on a leaf that fell off the tree on the first evening of Muharram.

ASHURA The last day of Muharram is called Ashura. After the ceremonial re-enactment of the death of Hussein, the women begin preparing a feast for the men and children. The whole village or family will gather at nightfall for a huge feast in honor of the landing of Noah's Ark. The mourning surrounding the death of Hussein is replaced by festivities to celebrate the perpetuation of humankind.

The Moslems, like the Christians and Jews, believe that Noah gathered two of every animal in the world and built an ark to sustain them through the great flood. When the flood came, all of the creatures of the earth were destroyed except those on the ark. Noah and his crew survived on the ark for 40 days, landed on dry ground and began a new life. The Moslems believe that Noah's landing deserves recognition and celebrate by feasting on Ashura.

The Grand Mosque of Mecca where hundreds of thousands of Moslems converge every year to perform the hajj. Mecca was the place where Prophet Mohammed was born, where he grew up and where the Holy Koran inspiration was revealed to him.

RAMADAN

Every year, Moslems around the globe observe the holy month of Ramadan by fasting during the day and eating or drinking only after the sun has set. The act of fasting proves their devotion to Mohammed and Allah. It also builds self-discipline and instills compassion for those less fortunate. Ramadan occurs once a year during the 9th month of the Moslem lunar year.

The holy month occurs at a different time each year because the cycle of the Moslem lunar year is not consistent with the calendar year. If Ramadan occurs during the cooler months of winter, Moslems do not suffer extensively from the lack of food or drink. During the hot summer months, however, it is very difficult to fast for an entire day. Sometimes the elderly and sick will die while fasting in observance of the holy month. When the fasting causes death, Moslems believe the deceased has died with Allah's blessing. In fact, Moslems consider it an honor to die during Ramadan.

EID AL-FITR

Eid al-Fitr is the "breaking of the fast" which occurs at the end of Ramadan. Moslems celebrate this three-day holiday by feasting and spending saved money. The wealthy Iraqis stay at home during Eid al-Fitr and invite friends and relatives over for feasts. The less wealthy Iraqis, predominantly those in the rural areas, purchase new clothes and dine with their richer friends.

MAULID AN-NABI

Maulid an-Nabi is a Moslem holiday that celebrates the approximate birthday of the Prophet Mohammed. The holiday occurs on the 11th day of the third Moslem month. On this holiday the older Moslems tell stories and legends about the birth of Mohammed.

When Mohammed was born, 7,000 angels brought heavenly dew to the earth in a golden urn and presented it to Mohammed's mother. Mohammed was bathed in the heavenly dew to perpetuate eternal cleanliness. As the child was born, every creature on the earth proclaimed, "There is no god but Allah and Mohammed is his Prophet." Legend says that the baby Mohammed had visitors from all over the land. The visitors were unable to look at Mohammed because his angelic face was brighter than the sun.

EID AL-ADHA

Eid al-Adha is the holiday in remembrance of Ishmael and his near-sacrifice by his father Abraham. The festival occurs on the 10th day of the 12th month of the Moslem year. On this day, Moslems visit the graves of their relatives and bring food to the poor in honor of Ishmael. According to legend, Abraham was told by Allah that he could prove his devotion by sacrificing his son Ishmael. Abraham tearfully prepared to kill his only son. As he was raising the knife to kill Ishmael, a voice from Heaven told Abraham to stop. Allah was satisfied with Abraham's faith and spared Ishmael. The Moslems celebrate Abraham's love for Allah and the survival of Ishmael every year on Eid al-Adha.

A goat or sheep is sacrificed to commemorate Abraham's love for God. The meat is then distributed to the poor and needy.

FESTIVALS CELEBRATING MARRIAGE AND BIRTH

The most exciting secular or non-religious celebration in Iraq is the wedding. The events surrounding the wedding start a few days before the marriage ceremony as relatives, friends and acquaintances host parties in honor of the couple. On the day of the actual wedding, the bride and groom are married in a small ceremony with only their relatives and closest friends present. After the ceremony, the wedding party parades through the streets of cheering residents to the site where the bride and groom consummate their marriage. The residents wait for the happy young couple while continuing to celebrate. When the newlyweds emerge from their home, the wedding festivities continue at a reception. The celebration often lasts until the early morning hours and is thoroughly enjoyed by all.

Another exciting festive occasion in Iraq is the celebration of the birth of a child. Three days after the birth the parents and the newborn are visited by friends and family. The visitors usually arrive with gifts for the child. The birth of a boy is celebrated with more intensity than the birth of a girl. Although women in Iraq have become more liberated in the past few decades, the Iraqis still feel that a girl is difficult and costly to raise as she will not contribute much to the family income when she is married. With the birth of each male child, superstitious rites are performed to provide protection throughout the boy's life. Visitors such as women without children or guests with blue eyes, the sign of a non-Iraqi, are discouraged from attending the birth festivities.

AL' KHATMA The religious festival that Iraqi Moslems take the most pride in is a child's reading of the Koran without mistakes. The children diligently study the Koran for a year or more in preparation for al' Khatma, or the

The Koran is reverently placed on a bookstand and normally read sitting down.

reading of the Koran. The reading is a very difficult task that only the dedicated can complete. The Moslems believe the reading of the Koran is the first step of many in receiving Allah's blessing. The true sign of a gift from Allah is a person's ability to truly understand the meaning of the Koran.

The boys and girls have separate ceremonies for al' Khatma. The boys read the Koran to the Moslem men and the girls do the same with the women. The ceremony is a very solemn occasion and an Iraqi child receives the undivided attention of his or her peers and elders while reading. When a child reads the Koran without error, he or she earns the title of *hafiz*.

After the child successfully reads the Koran, the solemn ceremony becomes an honorary festival in his or her honor. The men usually hold a luncheon for the boy while the women celebrate with an afternoon tea for the girl. Friends and relatives of the *hafiz* attend the festival and shower gifts and money on the honorary guest. All of the attendants dress in colorful clothes and spend the afternoon celebrating the child's accomplishment.

FOOD

THE CHIEF AGRICULTURAL products grown in Iraq are wheat, barley and rice. These products are staples in the Iraqi diet. The women in small Iraqi villages collect wheat and use it to make bread and other cereal-based products. Barley also serves as a main ingredient in many Iraqi dishes. Rice is usually cooked and eaten as a healthy main dish or side dish.

MEAT

The most important livestock in Iraq are sheep and goats. They are raised by nomadic and semi-nomadic groups to supply meat, milk, wool and skins. In small villages the butcher slaughters a sheep or goat every day. Villagers would hurry to his shop to claim the choice cuts for their dinner. Those who saunter into the butcher's shop later in the day will find only the remains of a carcass. Iraqis can cook almost every part of a sheep or goat. Delicacies include the kidneys, liver, brain, feet, eyes and ears. The meat is usually cut into small strips and cooked with onions and garlic for flavor. Iraqis also enjoy mincing the meat for a stew that is served with rice.

Meat can also be obtained from cows, chickens, camels and fish. In the past decade the production of processed chicken and fish has nearly doubled and will continue to grow with the construction of a multi-million dollar deep-sea fishing facility in Basra.

The Moslems in Iraq are not allowed to eat pork. The Islamic religion forbids it because the animal's eating habits are considered unhygienic.

Opposite: **An Iraqi farm worker inspects a vegetable marrow plant.**

Above: **Camels used to be a source of wealth and are still valuable animals today. Besides being hardy beasts of burden, they provide milk and meat for a variety of Middle Eastern foods.**

An itinerant fruit vendor sells bananas.

IRAQI KITCHENS

The kitchens in Iraq range from modern ones with microwave ovens to primitive rooms without running water or electricity. The regional location of a house is an indicator of the style and modernity of a kitchen.

For the most part, kitchens in village homes are quite simple. Many Iraqi villages lack running water for cooking. The women collect water from the river and heat it to kill the bacteria prior to the preparation of food. During the Gulf War, Allied bombing cut electricity and running water to many of the small villages and towns. People were forced to return to their primitive ways which resulted in deaths from impure water, food and poor hygiene.

Wealthy residents in the cities invariably hire a cook to prepare their food. Their kitchens are very modern with every electrical appliance that is necessary. The marketing is normally left to a servant or cook while the family merely supervises its preparation. Meals are eaten in a separate dining room, and as a result, family members rarely visit the kitchen.

FASTING

The fourth pillar of Islam is the observance of Ramadan. During this month, Moslems fast during the day and eat at night. To many outsiders of the faith, the practice of fasting is difficult to comprehend. Why must the Iraqi Moslems fast to prove their devotion to Allah? Moslems have several reasons for fasting during Ramadan.

Fasting enables the believer to think about religion, personal goals and loved ones. It also requires tremendous self-discipline to fast when there is an abundance of food. The Moslem who is fasting is constantly reminded of his or her dependence on Allah and his generous gifts. Finally, the fasting allows an Iraqi to develop compassion for those who do not have enough to eat. At the end of Ramadan, everyone gives alms and the wealthy usually invite the less fortunate into their homes to feast with them.

The meat of lamb and sheep are traditionally used for the preparation of special dishes during feasts and festivals.

FEASTING

The Iraqis express their joy and thanks to Allah by feasting. Two important feasts take place during the Moslem year; one to commemorate the end of Ramadan, and the other to celebrate the pilgrimage to Mecca.

To an Iraqi, a feast is a celebration equivalent to a party in the West. A feast is never a lonely affair nor is anyone left out. Neighbors, relatives and friends are invited to partake in the festivities.

The women spend hours preparing a meal which is enjoyed by all. Before and after a feast, there is usually singing, dancing and storytelling.

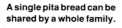

A single pita bread can be shared by a whole family.

COFFEE

Iraqis have a very interesting tradition in the preparation of coffee. The coffee beans are ground and then the drink is heated and cooled nine times before it is served. The Iraqis who drink their coffee this way firmly believe that they are removing all of the impurities from the imported product. This unusual tradition is observed mainly in the smaller villages and towns of Iraq. City-dwellers do not have the extra time to spend in preparation of this type of coffee.

The people of Iraq prefer their coffee sweetened with sugar and fresh cream or milk. Despite the personal preferences regarding the preparation of coffee, it is a social drink that is served in outdoor cafes, in restaurants and at parties to be enjoyed by all.

IRAQI DRINKS AND DESSERTS

The favorite Iraqi drinks are coffee and tea. Usually coffee and tea are served before and after meals because a substantial number of Iraqis do not like to mix food and drink.

Another favorite among the Iraqis is a cool, refreshing glass of ice water during the summer. Coca-Cola and other Western drinks are also very popular in the cities such as Baghdad and Basra.

The Moslem faith prohibits the intake of alcoholic beverages so the majority of Iraqis do not drink alcohol. Moslems also refrain from cooking with alcohol in case it does not evaporate during the heating process.

The Iraqis are renowned for their exquisite desserts. The favorites among Iraqis are pastries with powdered sugar and creamy fillings, thin pancakes or crêpes buried in layers of fruit and syrup, anything sweet with dates, and a special dessert called *ma'mounia*.

FAVORITE FOODS

A true Iraqi meal lives up to the term "feast." During a meal, there may be several appetizers, soups, salads, main dishes and desserts to choose from. With so many choices, an Iraqi meal often resembles an American restaurant!

A favorite Iraqi feast starts out with grilled kebab as an appetizer. Kebab is grilled meat (chicken or beef) and vegetables placed on a skewer for serving. The meat or vegetables are removed from the skewer with the hands. A popular soup is chicken noodle with herbs. Rather than using a spoon, the Iraqis usually pick up the bowl and drink the soup.

The main course of an Iraqi meal is always simple but delicious. The favorite entrée is boiled lamb with rice. Iraqis also enjoy roasted chicken and grilled beef.

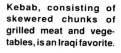

Kebab, consisting of skewered chunks of grilled meat and vegetables, is an Iraqi favorite.

In Iraq, the salad often follows the main course. Two popular salads are eggplant in meat sauce and sliced tomatoes. Along with the salad, the Iraqis serve *khubaz* which is a flat wheat bread. The bread is buttered and topped with a fruit jelly.

A FAVORITE IRAQI DESSERT

Ma'mounia was first made for a caliph during the 9th century. The caliph asked his cook to create a sumptuous dessert worthy of a king. The pudding that was created still remains a favorite among the Iraqi people. The following is the recipe for four servings of *ma'mounia*.

3 cups of water
2 cups of sugar
$1/_2$ cup of sweet butter
1 cup of semolina
1 teaspoon of lemon juice
1 teaspoon of ground cinnamon
Whipped cream

Place the sugar and the water in a large saucepan and stir constantly over low heat until the sugar dissolves. While adding the lemon juice, bring the mixture to a boil. After the syrup boils, reduce the heat and let it simmer until the syrup slightly thickens (about 10 minutes).

In another saucepan, melt the butter and add the semolina. Stir until the semolina is lightly fried. Pour in the syrup and stir constantly. Let the mixture simmer for another 10 minutes. Remove the dessert from the heat and let it cool for 20 minutes.

Spoon the *ma'mounia* into individual bowls. Place a large dab of whipped cream on top and then sprinkle the dessert with cinnamon.

THE EID AL-FITR FEAST

The end of the Moslem month of Ramadan is celebrated by feasting on Eid al-Fitr. After a month of fasting during the daylight hours, the Moslems look forward to the elaborate feast on Eid al-Fitr. The women solemnly prepare the feast for themselves, the men and the children of the community. The holiday is celebrated with intense fervor in the small villages and towns of Iraq.

The main dishes for a feast in an Iraqi village of approximately 300 people are one or two cows and five to seven grown sheep. The throats of the animals are slit and the insides are removed on the morning of the feast by one of the village men. The organs of the animals are prepared in a special way and the rest of the animal is roasted over a charcoal fire. The meat is usually cut into relatively small pieces and then mixed with vegetables or rice for serving.

When the feast is prepared, the village gathers in one large room to enjoy the meal. It is not uncommon for the men to sit on one side of the room or to move to an entirely different room to eat their meal. In a wealthy family servants are responsible for serving the feast. In more modest households, the women must prepare and serve the feast.

A friendly shopkeeper waits to serve a customer in his grain and spice shop.

TABLE MANNERS AND ETIQUETTE

The Iraqis have very strict rules concerning table manners and etiquette. Many of the rules apply specifically to eating, but others are equally important in everyday life.

GENERAL RULES OF ETIQUETTE

1. Iraqis always shake hands when greeting each other. If a man is greeting a woman, the woman extends her hand first to indicate that she wants to shake hands.
2. It is considered very rude to turn one's foot outward while talking to another. Iraqis will be extremely offended if someone turns the sole of his or her foot toward them.
3. If an Iraqi gives another a gift, it is always accepted with both hands and opened in the absence of the benefactor.
4. Iraqi men always stand when women enter the room and open doors for the women. All Iraqi citizens stand when an older person enters or leaves a room.
5. If someone praises an Iraqi's possession, such as a vase or small sculpture, the Iraqi will usually insist that the person have it. Therefore, it is proper etiquette to refrain from lavishly praising another's possessions.

TABLE MANNERS

1. Iraqis are very offended if someone uses his or her left hand while eating. For traditional reasons, the left hand is considered unclean by the Iraqis.
2. It is considered proper for only one person to pay the bill in a restaurant. Iraqis are embarrassed by the American tradition of equally splitting the bill among all the parties.
3. When an Iraqi has a dinner party or feast, he or she prepares an abundance of food. In order to appear polite, the guests usually attempt to eat everything in front of them.
4. It is not considered rude in Iraq to eat food quickly or without utensils. Rather, it is a sign to the host or hostess that the food is delicious.
5. Iraqis are extremely offended if a family pet such as a dog comes near the table while they are eating.
6. After eating a meal, the Iraqis lavishly praise the meal and the delightful preparation of the food.
7. When attending a meal prepared by someone else, an Iraqi will invariably bring a small gift to the host as a gesture of gratitude.

Friday lunch in convivial surroundings.

TRIPS TO THE MARKET

The cities and villages of Iraq are filled with small markets selling food. The markets are often part of a group of markets called a bazaar. The bazaars sell everything from delicious foods to beautiful handmade crafts. Within each market, however, the only items up for sale are edible.

The most successful markets sell fruits, vegetables, spices or fresh meat. In the small villages and towns, the men do the marketing after consulting with the women about which products to buy from the merchants. Women of these villages consider it a disgrace to appear in the public market or bazaar. Therefore, the markets and bazaars are brimming with servants, children and men.

EATING OUT

One of the true pleasures in Iraqi cities is dining out in one of the fine restaurants or cosy outdoor cafes. The restaurants provide food from all lands to their Iraqi diners and the cafes supply small servings in a wonderful atmosphere to their patrons. The Iraqis enjoy spending their afternoons sitting among friends in one of the outdoor cafes. Friends gather together to sip coffee, nibble on sweets and exchange gossip. On a hot day the cafes provide cold lemonade and water under large umbrellas or awnings. The regular customers of the outdoor cafes are often older gentlemen who spend a relaxing afternoon watching their fellow Iraqis hurry to work or leisurely shop in the bazaars.

REGIONAL FAVORITES

Topography and weather play a major role in determining the favorite foods of a particular region. These factors traditionally restrict Iraqis' choice of fresh foods to those that are available to them in their region. Modern transportation, however, has widened the choice.

THE TIGRIS AND THE EUPHRATES RIVERS The residents of the areas surrounding the two main rivers of Iraq are blessed with a daily selection of fresh fish. Another favorite food in the region is milk from the *jamoosa*, or water buffalo. The *jamoosa's* milk is rich and is used to make yogurt and butter. The yogurt is prepared by cooling the fresh milk overnight, scraping off the top layer and adding a yogurt starter. Within hours, the yogurt is ready for eating, cooking or diluting with water for a delicious drink.

THE NORTHERN COUNTRY The Iraqis of the northern regions, including the Kurds, enjoy eating meat from cows or chickens. Cows receive more nourishment in the cooler north and live longer, healthier lives. In turn, the meat and milk from these cows is delicious and rich. The women of the northern regions prepare homemade tomato paste from the abundant homegrown tomatoes. Another regional delicacy is goat's milk and cheese.

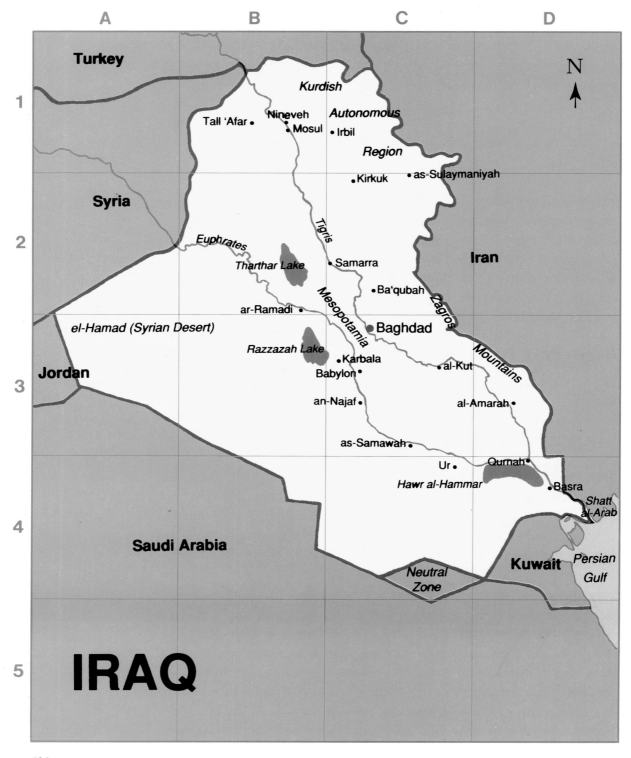

Turkey

A B C D

N

Kurdish

Tall 'Afar • • Nineveh
• Irbil
• Mosul

Autonomous

Syria

Region

• Kirkuk • as-Sulaymaniyah

Euphrates

Tharthar Lake

Tigris

• Samarra

Iran

• Ba'qubah

Mesopotamia

ar-Ramadi •

el-Hamad (Syrian Desert)

• Baghdad

Zagros

Razzazah Lake

• Karbala

• al-Kut

Jordan

Babylon •

Mountains

an-Najaf •

• al-Amarah

as-Samawah •

Ur • Qurnah •

Hawr al-Hammar

• Basra

Shatt al-Arab

Saudi Arabia

Kuwait

Persian Gulf

Neutral Zone

IRAQ

al-Amarah   D3
al-Kut   C3
an-Najaf   C3
ar-Ramadi   B2
as-Samawah   C3

Babylon   C3
Baghdad   C3
Ba'qubah   C2
Basra   D4

el-Hamad   A3
Euphrates   B2

Hawr al-Hammar   D4

Irbil   C1

Karbala   C3
Kirkuk   C2
Kurdish   Autonomous
    Region   C1

Mesopotamia   C2
Mosul   B1

Nineveh   B1

Qurnah   D4

Razzazah Lake   B3

Samarra   C2
Shatt al-Arab   D4

Tall 'Afar   B1
Tharthar Lake   B2
Tigris   B2

Ur   C4

Zagros Mountains   C3

—— **International Boundary**
● **Capital**
● **City**
✕ **River**
◗ **Lake**

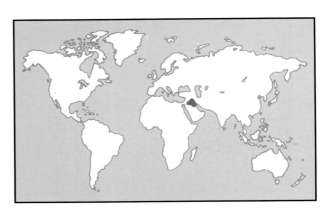

QUICK NOTES

AREA
173,588 square miles

POPULATION
16,278,000

CAPITAL
Baghdad

OFFICIAL NAME
Al-Jumhariya Al-Iraqiya

TERM FOR CITIZENS
Iraqis

FORM OF GOVERNMENT
Independent republic

OFFICIAL LANGUAGE
Arabic

NATIONAL ANTHEM
Al-Salam Al-Jumhuri

NATIONAL FLAG
Three horizontal bands—red, white, black—with three green stars on the middle white band.

MAJOR RIVERS
Tigris and Euphrates

MAJOR RELIGION
Islam

SECTS OF ISLAM
Shiite
Sunni

HIGHEST POINT
Zagros Mountains (11,910 feet)

MAJOR LAKE
Hawr al-Hammar

CURRENCY
Dinar
(US$1 = 0.31 dinars)

MAIN EXPORTS
Oil, dates, wheat, barley, rice, tobacco

LEADERS IN POLITICS
King Faisal I—king of Iraq (1921–33)
King Ghazi—king of Iraq (1933–39)
King Faisal II—king of Iraq (1948–58)
Brig. Abdul Karim Kassem—prime minister (1958–63)
Col. Abd as-Salam Arif—president (1963–66)
Gen. Abd ar-Rahman Arif—president (1966–68)
Maj. Gen. Ahmad Hassan al-Bakr—president (1968–79)
Saddam Hussein—president, prime minister and head of the armed forces (1979–present)
Tariq Aziz—foreign minister for Iraq who made headlines during the Gulf War

MOSLEM HOLIDAYS
Ramadan
Eid al-Fitr
Muharram
Maulid an-Nabi
Eid al-Adha

GLOSSARY

Assyrians	Ancient inhabitants of Assyria, a kingdom in northern Mesopotamia.
caliph	A title for the head of a Moslem state.
cuneiform writing	System of writing used extensively in Mesopotamia and Persia; the characters used in writing have a wedge-shaped appearance
hafiz	The title an Iraqi child earns after reading the Koran without error.
Kab'ah	The House of God in Mecca, to Moslems all over the world.
Kurds	A Sunni Moslem national minority with their own language and customs.
Ramadan	The ninth month of the Islamic calendar; a time of atonement and fasting.
sheikh	Honorary title of head of a tribe or clan.
ziggurat	An ancient Mesopotamian temple tower consisting of a lofty pyramidal structure with many stories.

BIBLIOGRAPHY

Bratman, Fred: *War in the Persian Gulf*, Millbrook Press, Brookfield, CT, 1991.

Childs, N.: *The Gulf War*, Rourke, Vero Beach, FL, 1991.

Foster, Leila M.: *Iraq*, Childrens Press, Chicago, 1990.

Salzman, Marian and O'Reilly, Ann: *War and Peace in the Persian Gulf: What Teenagers Want to Know*, Peterson's Guides, Princeton, NJ, 1991.

INDEX

PICTURE CREDITS
Christine Osborne: 4, 5, 6, 8, 16, 18, 19, 22, 27, 31, 32, 36, 39, 40, 41, 44, 46, 48, 49, 51, 55, 56, 58, 59, 60, 61, 63, 64, 65, 67, 68, 69, 70, 71, 79, 80, 82, 83, 84, 86, 87, 89, 95, 96, 101, 102, 104, 106, 112, 114, 115, 120, 122

Hajah Halijah: 108
Hunt Janin: 52
Jamie Simson: 1, 9, 10, 11, 13, 17, 38, 42, 43, 45, 50, 54, 57, 62, 73, 88, 97, 103, 109, 120
Reuters/Bettmann: 23, 24, 25, 26, 28, 29
The Image Bank: 7, 12, 15, 21, 34, 35, 47, 66, 76, 90, 91, 93, 113, 116